Wither
on the Vine

Roxolana
the
Artist

Pronunciation Guide

Names:

Arianrhod (AIR EE ANT RODE) : Callum's great aunt

Bhaltair (VAWL TAIR) : Callum, Eachann & Sabhinion's father

Cailleach Bheure (CAL EE YUH VER) : Celtic Goddess

Cairneach (CARE-NECK) : Callum's corrupt uncle

Callum (CAL EM) : Younger brother of Eachann

Carrig: (CARE-IK) : Callum's best friend

Cliodhna (KLEE-NAW) : Celtic goddess of the sea

Amhran de Cogadh (OAR AWN JUH COE GAH): Song of war – Eachann's each uisge name

Creiddylad (CRAY DUH LAH) : Callum's corrupt aunt

Dougal (DOO GUL): One of Galanta's stepbrothers

Eachann (A HEN): Callum's brother

Each Uisge (EK WISK EE) : mythological name of Callum's people

Einoringen (AIN ORE INJ EN): Brehon and scholar

Fergus (FAIR GES) : Galanta's stepbrother

Galanta (GUH LANT UH) : the mate of Eachann

Gealain Greine (GAY LEN GREN) Gaelic for glittering sunshine, the translation of Meghan's nickname

Iolanthe (EYE O LANT EE): Selkie Queen

Lianth (LENTH): Oldest daughter of Mairead

Lir (LEER) : Celtic god of the sea

Langihwen (LON YI WEN): Aunt Arianrhod's ward and Callum's distant cousin

Mairead (MAR ED) : Villager, friend of Galanta's deceased mother

Mo chridhe fiadhaich (MAW CHREE FEE OT HIGH CH): My wild heart – Eachann's nickname for Galanta

Morrigan (MOOR I GEN) : Celtic goddess of war and bringer of death

Morthecainn (MOOR TUH KEN) : Callum's cousin

Mo stoirm (MAW STOORM): My storm – Galanta's nickname for Eachann

Luathchosach (LOO AH HOSS EF) : Callum's each uisge name

Rhona (ROWN A) : Village tavern maid and love interest of Galanta's stepbrothers

Riordan (ROAR DAN): Each Uisge Spymaster

Sabhinion (SEV EE NEE UN) : Callum's sister

Other words:

Bean Sidhe (BAN-SHEE): Banshee. Ancient Celtic harbingers of death.

Ceilidh (KAY LEE): a Celtic party or celebration

Geas (GACE): a form of curse, a personal obligation placed on someone by the gods or magical creatures

Kinkcough (KINK KOFF): whooping cough

Leannan (LEE UH NAWN): Scots Gaelic for sweetheart

Machair (MACK-UH): grasslands in the Outer Hebrides

Maslin (MAZ-LIN): Flour mixture used in the dark and middle ages that was a mixture of wheat, barley, rye and other grains.

Thrapple (Pronounced like apple with a thr): A charm to protect against whooping cough, made from the larynx of a goose. Curved into a small circle and filled with stones.

Tuatha de Danaan (TOO-AH DAY DAN-UN): another name for the fae or elven folk of the Celtic islands

Contents

Prologue

My stepfather told me my green darkness killed my mother.

He said the old magic tainted my veins and must be bled out with penitence and a crown of nettles.

I bowed my head and knelt on the cold flagstone of the village chapel.

I swallowed the stale crust of bread the priest claimed was the body of his god.

I've spent my life beaten and broken and beseeching. But my heart never faltered. It was waiting for the thunder of his hooves and the wave of his fury. It was waiting for his words and his redemption.

The demons never leave me. They're borne of the blood I've spilt and they writhe beneath the surface of my skin.

When he wrapped his arms around me, I didn't feel the welts on my back or the scars in my heart. I was wholly his and he was wholly mine.

A golden prince of the sea and a witch with the forest in her veins. We were destined to be mortal enemies but fell in love instead.

I don't know how I'm still alive. Not after carrying around his absence for a thousand years. Not after recovering his broken body and giving him the princely burial he deserved. Not after losing our child and myself to blood and sorrow.

My green darkness killed him too.

When I first saw him, I thought the prince was like the dark sun that made people either tremble at its power or bask in wonder.

All the shiny parts of him flickered in his eyes.

Instinctively, I knew he was my enemy. It was the way he held himself. Apart and watching. The double sword hilts that rose from behind his shoulders confirmed my theory.

None of that mattered.

From the moment I met his eyes and saw the icy blue fury of the sea, I wanted nothing more than to hear the rumble of his laughter in my ear.

I wanted to know if it sounded like the fractured echo of the tide or the cold gleam of distant stars.

I sensed no danger in my heart, and my wild magic spiraled and bloomed, calling to his.

And so I rose to my feet and opened the door to my kind's greatest enemy.

This is the story of how we found and lost each other. And found each other again.

Chapter One

Galanta

Outer Hebrides Islands, 962 A.D.

O nce upon a time, I counted my life in summers.

Now I count my life in winters. The winters that have passed since I took the oath of my family. The winters that have passed since I lost my mother. The winters that have passed since my magic was silenced and bound. The winters that have passed since I first felt the lash of my stepfather's strap on my back.

I am a cunning woman. Like my mother, and her mother before her, I serve the goddess Morrigan. Her service is not for those who lack courage. She brings me dreams of darkness and death, of drowning in salt and sea, of fire and blood. For thousands of years, the women of my family have taken her protection and practiced their craft. We are born with her stamp on our skin – a birthmark just above our breast. My mother compared mine to the wings of a raven.

I see the runes in the leaves of the trees and know when the blackthorn winter will bring howling winds and bitter cold. I see the ripples in the scrying pool within the sacred grove of rowan and birch and know when the wolves of famine and want and sickness will descend on our village.

I am the last of my kind.

When I seek my own fate, the scrying pool shows only fire and darkness. My mother's last words were ones of warning. She told me I was born of joy and tragedy, that it shaped the walls of my soul and the chambers of my heart. She told me my obstinacy and rebellion would make my journey hard-fought and hard-won.

The ancient pendant became my burden to bear when I was barely a woman. The quartz is dusky gray with age, something powerful and primordial. When my mother slipped it over my head, she admonished me to keep its light hidden. She said the flickering I glimpsed within its depths should be banished from my mind as something perilous.

The quartz warms to my touch when I cup it in the palm of my hand. The flickering lights become more visible every day, as if an entire storm is trapped within it. There are other omens of things to come. The dreams that are never gentle. The ravens that roost in the tree at the village crossroads and flap in my wake as I pass.

My mother taught me all the curings she knew. Those of herbs and nine knots and midwifery. I loved her as much as I feared her. She was the only parent I knew until she wed my stepfather. He and his sons moved into our cottage and brought the black smoke, hot iron smell of their forge.

I know the magicks to heal. Or harm if need be. I've never used those darker spells – not because I don't have enemies. I haven't used them because they are dangerous. According to my mother, wielding those spells will throw open wide the door for the eldritch god. He wrestles against his imprisonment, and the crystal I wear around my neck is the only protection against loosing his wrath upon our island.

When she gave her life for mine, she left me alone with my newly acquired family. They are blacksmiths and hunters and have their own kind of mastery over nature that calls for conquest rather than communion. They bend the elements to their will instead of honoring the circle that binds us all together.

They tolerate my presence in their home because otherwise they would starve and wear nothing but rags. My stepfather has claimed his capacity for love lies in the village churchyard and my stepbrothers are churlish louts who are too fond of ale.

Though I've never spoken of what happened in the grove on that day, my stepfather blames me for her death. I have the scars on my back to prove it. When he grows bored of tormenting me, he delivers me to the priest for punishment of the wickedness he claims I harbor. The priest, Father Mulcahy, is only too eager to banish me to a cell with no sustenance for days on end and flay my skin open. His instrument of torture has a spiked end and makes the blood in my veins rise and bloom from below the surface.

I know I will never escape this place. The sea beckons me to surrender and leave it all behind, but I refuse to give those who want me gone the satisfaction. Day in and day out I resign myself to my fate as I sit at my loom and weave stories in my head of a life more charmed than mine.

I am only invited over thresholds out of necessity. Father Mulcahy and his church have sowed seeds of distrust and suspicion. My fellow villagers only turn to me for help when they have exhausted the limits of prayer to no avail. That is when they consent to my use of cures and simples.

My mother instructed me in the use of the family grimoire, and she paid the price for my arrogance and ignorance. When my quest for more power and knowledge wakened the eldritch Forest Lord, she slit open her wrists so I wouldn't be taken. I watched the blood leak from her veins, like dark ink, seeping across the bed of brittle leaves and strewn needles.

I have denied my heritage and squelched my magic since that ill-fated day. Even though the grove whispers at moonrise, begging me to untether the depths of my power, I ignore it. Those whispers are perilous because they ignite something within the depths of the crystal that pulses against my skin. If I succumb to the temptation of those whispers, death and destruction will follow. No one else need pay the price for my covetous nature.

Every night the crystal burns a hole through my woolen shift. It's speckled like I've stood in the wake of sparks from my stepfather's forge. I feel the claws of the eldritch king around my throat, like the roots of his trees, dragging me to my grave.

Chapter Two

Eachann

"It is time you wed. We need to secure the succession. Your mother and I have waited long enough for you and your brother to give us bairns."

I carefully lean away from the table. "I'm not averse to marriage. I just haven't met the right woman. I want a true mate, not someone who bears my sigil because of what being aligned to our family will bring them. Surely you understand why I want the kind of love story shared by my parents."

"You must abandon your affinity for the bard tales, Eachann. I have spoken to the selkie queen. Her eldest daughter is of age and we both desire a more formal alliance between our kingdoms. Your mother and I began our love story as enemies, and who's to say you will not find what you seek with this princess?"

We've had a fragile truce with the selkies since we took back the southern islands three hundred years ago. "Are you trying to arrange my marriage, Father?"

Well over a thousand years ago, I laid down my harp and exchanged it for a sword and scepter. But the music is still buried somewhere deep within my soul. I know it will brazen its way to the surface if I ever meet the one destined for me. My father isn't wrong - the selkie princess could very well be my soulmate. We were acquainted with each other in our long-ago childhood, but those visits ended when our kingdoms sought out the same hunting grounds. I remember her aversion to attention, and the peek of her white gold hair from behind her mother's skirts.

If she is not the one who will awaken my music, it will stay hidden. As each uisge, vows made during the sigil ceremony are exclusive and binding. Those who violate the bond have a history of meeting terrible ends. We are encouraged to explore our sexuality in all its forms, but once we are wed, any liaisons outside of that union are strictly discouraged if not outright forbidden. Even if we meet the one that is destined for us.

"By all accounts, she's a lovely woman poised to rule her kingdom when her mother sails to the west."

The soothing words soften the sudden blow, and I am grateful to my mother for her interjection. I know I am just another unintentional, but necessary, casualty of my father's blunt political manipulation.

I ruefully shake my head. Even if the princess and I are complete opposites or cannot bear to be in the same room with one another, my father will push this union. If I mate with the selkie princess in her human form, he'll get what he wants. An heir and access to their vast realm of influence. Our hunting grounds will expand, and more territory will be within each uisge control. "Invite them here so we may become better acquainted."

He throws me a sharp nod and a benevolent grin before he turns to my mother.

Callum chuckles quietly beside me. "Ye seem disconcerted, brother."

His eyes are creased with mirth, and I wish I could see him squirm on a hook like this. "Should I have suspected this was in the making?"

"He's wanted an alliance with the selkies for eons. But ye cannae have predicted this. I dinnae envy ye being commanded to wed a lass neither of us remembers."

"She liked building things in the sand and cried when the tide washed them away. It was the only time she left the shelter of her mother's skirts."

"I remember. The starfish ye found and presented to her finally stopped her tears." He stands and clasps my shoulder. "We'll find out soon enough what she's truly like."

"Should I procure a gift?"

He cocks his head and guffaws. "A gift? Like the starfish? Don't be so ridiculously sentimental, brother. Don't all women love gems? Just give her one of those. We have plenty of them in the treasury to choose from. Why expend additional effort for a bride ye needn't woo?"

Callum never indulges in courtship. He keeps his liaisons free of expectations and teases me for what he calls my serial monogamy. "She'll expect me to woo her. And she should. Even if it's an arranged marriage. I should give her a gift that results from my own endeavors, not something I choose from the kingdom's coffers."

"So ye'll waste the effort and woo her? Even though she's a sure thing and like ye willnae have a choice in this?"

"A woman is never a sure thing, brother. You know this, despite all your escapades. And the wooing isn't a guarantee. That's not what wooing's about. It's to convey respect and appreciation. Doubtless of the reason, Father will give me no choice. He and her mother will expect me to woo her."

"Mother won't let him pressure ye if there's no possibility of love. Or if she sees the union will make ye miserable."

I sigh. "You know that's not true. She only holds so much sway over him. I'm to be the pawn of the throne in this."

He shakes his head. "Ye're wrong. Though he wears the crown, ye know who holds the power behind it. He'd do nearly anything to make her smile. And he lives in fear of her glares and tears."

"The grandest love story ever told." We chorus in unison.

Our mother was a hostage and the daughter of my father's greatest enemy. After she bested him in a swordfight and slapped him on the ass with the flat of her weapon, he fell in love. Or so he likes to recount with a fond smile and eyes full of stars.

"I'm just glad ye're the one he picked and nae me."

My twin brother avoids emotional attachments to his lovers like the plague, so I'm not surprised at his relief or lack of sympathy. He's stoic when he's not fucking and is a trifle arrogant about his responsibility to protect our kingdom.

There are so many ways I can give him his comeuppance, but his unholy fear of spiders is the one I inwardly cackle over.

"Your day will come sooner than you expect it to. I wouldn't be so cavalier about my impending nuptials."

"Better ye than us, Cailin Ban."

I throw a chunk of bread in Carrig's direction. When he and Callum want to annoy me, they call me *that*. Golden girl. It's their way of poking fun at the way women swoon over my hair.

"Will ye make a braid for her to climb up to yer window?"

I glare at Callum. "It's not that long."

"Mayhap he'll let her plait it herself. He won't even need to woo her; he can just blind her with all that *glorious sunlight*." Carrig simpers the last two words.

"Your day will come too." I remind him with a glower.

He crosses his arms. "But my union won't be arranged, and I'll have my pick."

He won't have his pick if our sister has any control over his choice. Sabhinion is a prickly subject with Carrig. Callum and I know she's always been infatuated with him, but he seems oblivious to it. He's weirdly protective of her, even though she's a wee bean sidhe, and he speaks of her as if she's his sister as well.

She grumbles about it constantly. She'll definitely confront him if he chooses anyone but her.

"Aren't you fortunate?"

He frowns. Likely because he hears my sarcasm. "I'm not bound by the same duties, but I have my own legacy to live up to."

Callum and I exchange a knowing glance. Our friend is the illegitimate son of the Kraken King. A king who has no sons other than him and no one to leave his throne to. He's yet to acknowledge Carrig.

There was a flurry at court when his parentage was revealed. The seers didn't even think a kraken and each uisge union was possible. His mother was the last female born to an each uisge before Sabh. She wed one of our grandfather's younger brothers, but for hundreds of years their union was infertile. When she became round with child, the kingdom was overjoyed.

All seemed well until Carrig transformed into his beast form for the first time. He not only had our fearsome hooves and eyes full of cold fire, but his body was also covered in tentacles, like vines. His mother confessed her adultery and his sire, the man he'd been raised to believe was his father, murdered her for the betrayal. Carrig doesn't know if the Kraken King is even aware of him, or if he was born out of love.

The tragic tale of his mother and father are why we are discouraged from straying outside the sigil bonds. Each uisge are possessive and envious once the bond is formed. A conquest outside of the union is seen as disrespectful.

"I'll do my duty. If it galls me, or she's intolerable, I'll find solace elsewhere."

"And risk her singing you into an eternal sleep because she refuses to share? Or end up like my parents? You'll be expected to remain true to your vows – no matter what sort of affinity is between you. You know this. And you're too cocksure. What if she finds you intolerable?"

It's not sheer conjecture. There is the very real possibility my selkie bride will use her powers on me if I betray her. Depending on how proud she is.

"She'll find me more than tolerable." I smirk. "Especially with my hair like golden sunlight. And where there is a will there is a way."

Carrig and Callum both roll their eyes at me before filling their arms with the half-full wineskins. "Come. It's time to celebrate or commiserate. Your choice."

Chapter Three

Galanta

My mother taught me much before we lost her,
and her lessons have held me in good stead.
She swore by the sign of the raven. She would often
tap the winged birthmark above my breast and remind

me that ravens were the midnight couriers of the
Morrigan and brought death and desolation in their
wake.

There were ravens perched all along the stone wall
encircling the village this morning. They flitted back
and forth between the village enclosure and the two
trees that stand at the crossroads. I swung my basket
in their direction and when they cawed in response
it sounded as if they were mocking me. The hag of
winter is slowly releasing her hold on us, and the change
of season means there are even more in need of my
medicine.

Some of the village children have succumbed to a
persistent cough. Even the thatcher's children, who all
wear thrapples around their necks, have been hacking
throughout the night. The priest insists the illness
is caused by evil spirits and fasting will draw them
out. Some of the village elders advise that passing the
diseased under the belly of a white horse will resolve the
affliction. I suspect it is kinkcough, passed onto us by
one of the sailors, and know neither of these things will
prove helpful. I hope the ravens aren't lingering about
to collect the souls of those who fight against the fever.
There have been so many afflicted this season, if I am to
have the red thread I need for curing, I must find rue.

One of the smallest boys has lain in his narrow bed, sweating and thrashing, for three days. His mother came to me last night, desperate. She knocked on the back door of our cottage, sneaking away under the guise of attending vespers. She said her prayers weren't working and she wondered if recanting her allegiance to the goddess was worth the life of her only son. Her husband is one of the fishermen who calls me naught more than a witch and she knew he'd be furious if he caught her.

I need to prepare a tincture of wormwood for the boy's fever, but my supplies are running low. I decided this morning that a foray into the woods that ring the grove is worth the risk of punishment I may face upon my return. My stepfather and stepbrothers have been toiling at the forge since we broke our fast this morning, and it's unlikely they'll take note of my absence.

The air has the sting of snow in it, and the sharp bite of the north wind swirls about my ankles. The coming weather hangs heavily, the scent of it raw and foreboding. I lengthen my stride to ensure I'm in front of the hearth when the fury of the sea hits the shore.

Despite the cold, the forest is a welcoming embrace. I feel closer to my mother's spirit in this place where she bartered her blood for my safety. I have never been afraid to step into the shadows of the trees, to place my hand against the towering strength and feel the pulse of sap against my fingertips like a steady heartbeat.

I'm able to find wormwood, elderberry and mugwort to replenish my stillroom. I'll need all of them and more if I'm to be armed against whatever is felling the children. The sun is sinking low, and I've finished with barely enough time to make my way back before dark. My stepfather is not a patient man when he is hungry, and I'll feel his wrath on my skin if I don't make haste. My stepbrothers follow his lead. Their shouting and preening are surely the reason they've yet to find women willing to tolerate them. Neither of them is married and they seem disinterested in pursuing anyone in skirts but the girl who serves them ale in the tavern on the wharf. I've seen her grimace when they come near, and I think she only tolerates their shenanigans for the bit of coin they slip in her pockets.

The priest is waiting at the crossroads when I emerge from the shelter of the trees. "What have you been at, girl?"

I gather my courage and do my best to appear submissive. "Simply gathering herbs, Father."

"There'll be no dispensation of your remedies to the god-fearing members of my flock. Prayer is all the remedy required."

If prayer were all that is required, the churchyard would not be full of newly turned soil. I can't resist the urge to befuddle him. "Am I not a member of your flock?"

"Unwed, wicked girls with wildness in their eyes are not members of my flock. You need more of the lash upon your back to beat the rebellion from you. You are not meek. Not as a woman should be."

"All I've ever wanted was to provide succor where it's needed. My mother taught me much, and I want to honor her legacy."

His lips curl into a sneer. "Your mother was naught but a witch, and you're no better. You'll come to no good and leave destruction in your wake. Your stepfather has tasked me with bringing you to heel."

"My mother wasn't a witch. She was a cunning woman and used her skill to keep us all hale and hearty." I take a deep breath and my simmering anger boils over. "And I am not a dog. Despite what my stepfather claims, I needn't be brought to heel."

"I agree," he snarls. "You are not a dog. You are an aberration. The knowledge you possess of the workings of nature and the human body was never meant to be the dominion of the weaker sex. I see it is time to have words with your stepfather again about your wickedness."

Whenever the priest complains to my stepfather, lashings are sure to follow. My back is a map of crevasses and scars already, and I know what to expect. In that moment, when the air from the descending punishment whistles past my ear, I go somewhere else in my head. To the cool velvet darkness of the trees.

"I'll not stop you." Any effort I make to bargain with this man will be futile.

"As if you could, foolish girl. I have the might of the lord on my side."

I make every effort to avoid the abhorrent priest. He claims to be a servant of his gospel but seems more concerned with the persecution of innocents. Especially women and those who still worship the old gods.

I bow my head in acknowledgment, falsely demure for his benefit. I remind myself that it will not help my cause to show more rebellion or attract more notice than I already have. "Yes, Father. I am an obedient servant of the gospel."

He shakes a finger at me, and even from my vantage point I can see the flecks of spittle in the corners of his mouth. "See that you remain so. The holy sight sees all your transgressions."

I hold back the shiver of premonition that courses down my spine at his words. I dip my head again and skirt around him, eager to escape his scrutiny.

When I arrive at our cottage, I sigh in relief to discover my family is still at the forge. I season the mutton stew with rosemary and thyme, stoke the hearth and lift my mother's mortar and pestle from the shelf. It is worn smooth, and I always feel closer to her when I use it. I use it to grind the herbs and set the rue up for dye-making. When I've finally finished replenishing my depleted stores and sweeping the day's dust with the broom I purified this morning, I take a seat before my loom.

I run my fingers over the weave, trying to discern a pattern. I don't know what spell this piece of cloth is intended to hold, but I'll at least imbue it with a charm for protection.

A shadow darkens the window and I glance up in fear because my stepfather has forbidden me to dispense cures in the daylight hours. I've felt the lash for my disobedience far too often. I'm raising my hand to signal the interloper around the side of the house, when I realize this is no ordinary visitor.

Even with the shaft of late afternoon sunlight obscuring my view, I know my visitor is not one of the villagers seeking a remedy. The figure is too broad and too tall and stands there, immobile in the half shadow. As if mesmerized.

When he steps closer, the hilts of the swords crossed over his back and the runes that crawl over his forearms broadcast his kin if not his identity. He is one of the changeling sea creatures the priest reviles and the village fears.

Chapter Four

Eachann

I traded our latest cache of pearls for leather and iron and a gift for my prospective selkie bride. My ship is waiting in the harbor, and I should be eager to leave this cursed place and return to it. Something compels me to stroll in the opposite direction.

A beam of afternoon sunlight cuts through the curtains fluttering in one of the cottage windows.

I catch a glimpse of a slender girl with hair like fire bent over her loom. That glimpse pulls me to her like a beggared fool. The music roars to life within me and nearly brings me to my knees. I want to howl with exasperation and disappointment. I haven't heard the notes in years, and now, when I am on the cusp of fulfilling a matrimonial obligation based on nothing more than duty, they flood my soul. The longing to let the riot of sound flow from my heart to the harp is overwhelming – and its resurrection can mean only one thing. That my mate is near.

I should make haste back to my boat. This village is not a safe place for our kind. But neither my beast nor I can withstand the call of our destiny.

Six millennia ago, when my grandfather sat on the throne, the truce was newly brokered, and we could walk these streets without fear. There were no priests or altars to the new god. The people still came to us for protection from the might of the sea and blessings over their catch.

Now they barely tolerate us. Most of them scurry away and make the signs to ward themselves against our evil. Their faces are filled with fear and revulsion, not respect and humility. On every holy day their new leader pounds his fist on his wooden pulpit and builds their loathing.

It is dangerous here and I am alone.

But the winter light spills through the window, illuminating this girl against the drab gray backdrop of her cottage. Her hair is the color of the blood moon, a beacon in the shadows. I cannot look away. As the melody of all that she is spills through my veins, I will her to open the casement and see me.

I don't feel the snowflakes landing on my shoulders. I don't notice the bitter wind skating over my exposed cheeks and the bridge of my nose. When she finally looks up from her loom, her eyes flare wide and her face flushes rosy and sweet.

When her eyes meet mine, brimming with all the colors of spring, I am lost. When she steps forward my heart cracks in two, a great and terrible rending, and I know half of it will be forever in her keeping. I know that the half remaining will beat for her and her alone.

How will I find the fortitude to bow to the yoke of duty when a woman such as she exists?

Just as I've willed her to do, she moves to the casement and swings it wide. I step forward in a daze and rest my elbows on the ledge. I brace myself against it so she won't see how I tremble at the sight of her. My bones feel like seawater, and my vision is blurred.

"What do you seek, sea creature?"

"I saw you at your loom and I couldn't look away."

"Are you daft? Or has too much ale impaired your vision? I am mortal and I know what you are."

I take her hands in mine, and the soul that has been buried in quiet darkness recognizes hers. Before she tugs them from my clasp, I see the crescent moons of dirt beneath her nails. Her veins are like the shadowed roots of trees, her blood the slow, bittersweet rise of sap.

I am saltwater and my power is in the crashing tide, and I am weak here where I cannot shift.

I know that she is mine. That our moments together will be stolen and brief. Clandestine and cloaked in night. That they will not be enough for either of us, but they will be all we have. She is mine to claim – the mate that will quiet the beast whose hooves are even now a cacophony within my chest. He knows her touch will soothe and quiet and make us whole.

"I am Eachann."

She drops my hands and steps away, her eyes searching mine. She takes a deep breath, as if she's gathering her courage, and steps forward again. Like a curious magpie whose attention is caught by something that gleams and shines.

"I am Galanta."

I would gladly plait my hair if she wanted to scale the walls to my tower. I would gladly grow my beard long enough to plait it too.

"You know what I am. Do you know all that I am?" Does she know I have cut down my foes with sword and teeth and the swift descent of my hooves? Does she know that I am more fearsome than gentle, more fierce than soft? That I bring chaos and storm and the sea that buries her kind and keeps their secrets forever? Does she know that I would forsake all of that for her?

"Yea. I have been warned against your kind all my life as cursed, unholy and evil. I don't know why you are here, and I know you shouldn't be. I know I should send you away instead of encouraging you or this conversation. The priest will make me the topic of his sermon if he sees me talking to you. He'll encourage my stepfather to put me in stocks for my disobedience. But I am inclined to pay little heed to the words of the priest. He has no love for my kind either and will find some other transgression worthy of chastisement if not this one."

"Your kind?" I sense no wild sea magic in her. I scent a trace of siren ancestry in her blood, but it is too faint for others to indict her. If she is not a siren, what manner of creature is she to ignite the wrath of the priest?

"I am an acolyte of the forest and a servant of Morrigan. As my mother was. And her mother before her. A descendant of generations of cunning women. According to the priest, I am an abomination who taints the sanctity of all those around me. I must tread as carefully as you. We are the same, you and I."

I cannot sense her magic because it is made of earth and forest. "You are not an abomination. And neither are my kind. Men like your priest revile those they fear. He fears you, and that is why he calls you such."

"I know this. But my knowledge changes nothing. In everything I must be cautious. Even now, I know he turns the village against me."

"I will not allow any harm to come to you." The vow echoes the fury rising in me, that any would dare threaten this woman I recognize as my mate. I will protect her with my immortal soul and break the bones of anyone who dares lay a finger on her into nothing more than brittle dust.

She laughs harshly. "There is nothing you or anyone else can do to prevent it. Especially if you insist on pursuing me and I allow it. The castigation and punishment will escalate because whatever we build between us will be beyond their ken. People fear that which they do not understand."

The quiet of dusk wraps around us and I get lost in the jade spark of her gaze. "We should not give them reason to persecute you."

"So we won't see each other again? You won't pursue me? I thought it was a course you were already decided upon." A dimple appears in her cheek and her mouth curls into a slight smile.

I shake my head. "I can no more stay away than I can breathe. Because I have no choice. Even now I am bound to you in blood and bone. You make my each uisge long to snatch you up and run away with you."

"Your passion should frighten me, but I'd willingly run away with anyone to escape this place. Even to the waves and salt of your kingdom. Even though it would part me from the earth. I would abandon this horrid place and never look back."

"Your family and your people are here. You would not be so rash."

"I would be so rash. My mother lies in the cold ground, and all I have left of her is my gift of spring and healing. The gift she shared and passed down to me. I fear even my gift will be taken from me because, as you said, it is feared. The priest watches and waits like a spider in its web for me to falter. My stepfather and stepbrothers are stern taskmasters in some things, but not in this. They will neither protect me nor challenge the priest. If he comes for me, they will be weak and spineless and will let him drag me away. Because though they'll never admit it, they fear me as well. I bear their fear in every scar. It is why you find me here, readying myself to prepare the evening meal in the middle of the day instead of the grove."

"The grove?"

"The grove of birch and rowan that is a brisk walk from the village enclosure. It holds the heart of our people. They have all abandoned it because they are frightened of the repercussions such worship will wreak on their lives. Worse yet, they have forsaken it at the behest of the priest. He knows my obeisance is feigned."

"You have pledged your allegiance to the new religion."

She laughs bitterly. "Only out of necessity. I have often confessed to sins I do not own and bared my skin to the rod. I carry the welts like armor. I knew my life would soon change. For six moon cycles my dreams have been filled with the roar of sea and fire."

"Those dreams were an omen?"

"Yes. My mother always told me I was a child of both tragedy and joy. That it was wrought in my soul. She said

I would wield them both. And now her dream has proven true."

"How would you describe me? Am I to be of tragedy or joy?"

She leans forward again and my breath hitches in my chest when her hand cups my jaw. I close my eyes at the feel of the calloused pads of her fingers sifting through the day's growth of beard.

"Open your eyes."

I obey her. I'm helpless against the gentle plea in her voice and the music spirals through me again.

"I think you'll become both my joy and my tragedy. But I will take the destruction if it comes. Because I think I want the joy as well. I've had little of it in my life. And mayhap it is the chance for love."

I place my hand over hers. "I vow I will not destroy you. I would sooner take my own life."

"Do not make vows that tempt the old gods. They are both petty and cunning. Vow instead to be near to me whenever you can. To come to know my heart as you know your own."

I want to protest that I already know her heart. But as much as I will it to be so, I do not. She may now claim the half of me that knew only darkness, but I have yet to see her darkness. I have yet to see the depth of her wild magic.

"I vow I will come to know your heart as my own. I will meet you in your grove in tomorrow's gloaming."

The gloaming is when all things are possible. Even the union of enemies.

"I will see you then." She rises to her toes and the softness of her lips dances along the jaw she just held. I want to catch her hand and pull her closer.

She slides away with a wry smile, and I watch her turn on her heel and disappear into the drab gray cottage once again.

I stand there in the waning light. I can still feel the imprint of her kiss on my cheek.

"You've been mooning about like a besotted calf all morning. That's the second time I've gotten under your defenses. If you're lucky, it won't scar your pretty face, cailin ban."

Even his use of that despicable nickname can't quell my joy. Usually, I can hold my own against him. At least with my sword. But my mind drifts today. It's already in the grove of trees waiting for her.

"I met someone. And I hear music again."

He draws up and thrusts his sword into the ground. "I suspected as much. Ye've been humming and tapping yer fingers against the hilt of yer sword. 'Tis only when ye're set on a new conquest that ye're so distracted and so easily defeated."

"It's not a conquest."

"Who is she this time? And what makes ye believe she is so different from all the others?" He scowls and crosses his arms.

"She is from the village. And she is an outcast. She has scars on her wrists and across her brow. She confessed she wears them on her back as well. Her soul is fierce and strong and when I saw her for the first time my world stood still. So still I became dizzy with the wonder of it."

"And ye hear music again. Because of yet another human. Is this an infatuation because ye want to tup her or is it more? Ye have this reaction to every one of yer lovers."

"I'm fairly certain she is my mate. I've never heard music before. Not like this."

"Ye're certain she's your mate and it's not because you want to seduce an innocent? Maybe the music means nothing. Why must ye constantly endanger your life? Mayhap I tire of being both yer conscience and yer nursemaid. Havenae ye learned yer lesson? And shouldn't ye be focused on the selkie princess ye're to meet?"

The last time I was reeled in by a human, he had to rescue me.

"Nay, it's not that. This time feels different. She's beautiful, aye. But sharp too. Like the edge of my sword when I've just pulled it from the whetstone. Nothing about her is delicate, innocent, or easy. I wanted my harp as soon as I saw her."

He scoffs. "How is it different? She's still human. Ye're not. Her kind won't let ye be together. She'll lead ye a merry chase. Even if she is yer mate. And yer infatuation will upend all our father's plans."

"I believe she's nothing like the others. Not my other lovers and not her kind. There is magic in her veins that calls to mine. And she admitted she's not immune to me."

"A mortal tainted with magic is not a wise choice for yer affections."

I laugh bitterly. "I am helpless against the very thought of her. Already she haunts me. There is no choice."

"Ye've said that before. You give yer trust too easily."

My younger brother is always chastising me for giving those I meet the benefit of the doubt. For assuming everyone has the best of intentions. He's rescued me from my folly more times than I care to admit. He tells me I am more like one of the hounds than a fierce each uisge warrior. That my brash eagerness to please is more like that of a dog than a horse and I should have a lolling tongue instead of hooves. He tells me it is my bard's heart that craves the poetry of falling in love. But this girl with eyes of newly unfurled spring leaves and a spirit that is strong like the rowan and bends like the willow, is different.

"Her soul calls to mine and I cannot wait for the claiming. As soon as it can be arranged." I lean away and cross my arms over my chest.

"Well, ye're useless when ye're pursuing a wench. Especially a human one. And ye're always drawn to the ones who will nae be easily lured. Ye've a penchant for the wily, wary vixens, not the ones who spread their legs as soon as ye cast a smile in their direction."

"She's not just a chase. My beast rose in my chest, Callum. And you know our souls are buried too deep to call to anyone. His hooves beat in time to the music. You know how long it has been since I've wanted to compose a new song. The gods purposefully crafted us to recognize our mate and my beast spoke to me. He was furious and impatient when we scented her. He's never had that reaction. She is mine."

He sighs heavily and scrapes his hand across his face. "So, when's the wooing to begin? Will there be gifts like those ye intended to give yer selkie bride? And what of her? Is this yer last bid for freedom before you assume the yoke of responsibility?"

"I'll make amends with Father when I need to. But I cannot stay away."

Callum straightens. "It's dangerous. The village is no longer welcoming to our kind. If ye can't step away enough to be wary, I'll be the one who watches yer back."

I slap him on the shoulder. "Surely, they won't try anything in the daylight. Especially with you and your cadre at my back. I vow I'll be careful. Thank you, brother. This time you won't regret it."

He gives me a one-armed hug in return. "I shall make sacrifices to all the sea gods to ensure ye're not drawn and quartered and buried in the cold ground."

Sacrifices may persuade the fickle gods and goddesses to align themselves with my desire. Such protection may shield us from tragedy.

Callum has reason to be wary. The last woman I lost my heart to betrayed me. I barely escaped her father's harpoon. My brother never trusted her and followed me that day. His quick reflexes are the only thing that saved me from being cleaved in two.

Since that fateful day we have stayed away from the village and only made contact out of bare necessity. When there are things we need and we have things to barter for in return.

Until now. I can't stay away. If I don't wither away from her absence, my beast will. The beat of his hooves inside my chest has been incessant since we left her. She is the one who will tame him, like those ridiculous stories of maidens and unicorns.

Chapter Five

Galanta

My stepbrothers and stepfather were busy at the forge this day. Their faces are black with the soot of it. They usually leave me to my own devices and I am always supremely glad of their apathy.

"Why does the stench of the sea linger in our doorway, daughter?" My stepfather thunders as he crosses our threshold with a wrinkled nose.

"One of the fishermen had a cart full of cod he was hauling down the street." This is true. The smell may have left its residue on our doorstep. And it means I needn't mention my encounter with the Prince of Lir. As far as my stepfather and stepbrothers are concerned, such a meeting is cursed because the sea kingdom is poison to mortals.

I point to the table replete with bowls of pottage to distract him. I was able to trade a skein of blue yarn for a piece of salted mutton, and the dish has been absorbing the flavor in the iron cookpot all day. "Your evening meal has been prepared. There is mutton in the pottage tonight."

My stepbrother Fergus greedily rubs his hands together. "I grow weary of fish."

We all do. Most of our meals are provided by the sea that thunders just beyond the cliffs. The small farm holdings we have are a meager supplement to whatever the catch brings us. My family, and most of those in the village, rely on its bounty and resent the way we are beholden to it. My father and stepbrothers are not fishermen, but it is fishermen who exchange their catch for the tools they make. I manage to barter my weaving for vegetables, mutton, and the rare shank of beef from those who've managed to produce it, and scavenge nuts, berries and greens from the forest and heath so the fish don't comprise the entirety of our diet. My family despises what they deem the witchery part of my soul but are silently grateful for its intervention on their behalf.

My family scarves down the mutton stew and I gladly fill their bowls again. If they are sated, there are fewer questions. The cold winter nights when the sea and the wind are beating against our cottage are the longest and hardest. Those are the nights we go to bed with rumbling stomachs and short tempers. Those are the nights I usually feel the whip on my back.

"'Twas a good meal, Daughter." They all lean back in their chairs, their hands on their stomachs. Calm and replete. There will be no taunting or rod tonight. No more thrashing or banishment to the priest for the meting out of my penance.

"Yes, Sister. For once you have proven useful."

I ignore the way my stepbrother Dougal gloats. I know the lot of them would either consume nothing but raw fish or starve if I disappeared. The temptation to do just that, with none other than the prince of the creatures they despise, was strong today.

"You may venture into the forest tomorrow to gather your herbs." My stepfather's pronouncement is unexpected.

I had planned to commune with the grove tomorrow, with or without my stepfather's permission. But now I have it, there will be no one to hinder me from leaving the village. I can meet the prince at dusk with no fear of repercussion.

"My shelves are nearly bereft, thank you, Stepfather." I sense the herbs I gathered today will prove insufficient for my needs. Too many of the children in the village struggle to breathe with this new sickness, and many of the adults have a brittle cough and rheumy eyes as well. There are herbs besides feverfew that will help, and I know I can find them if I venture further into the forest.

"You are not to dispense herbs to those who have crosses etched above their lintels. I know I cannot stop you from healing small hurts, but your meddling will only make this plague worse."

This is one of the priest's newest endeavors. Those who have pledged to tithe more than half their harvest to the church have a cross carved into the wattle and daub of their homes. A tangible show of their support and a sacred ward against evil. Those homes have turned their backs completely on the old religion.

"I'll not dispense to anyone who doesn't ask for it."

"You'll stay away from the sick unless your services are specifically requested, daughter. I'll not have my hearth cursed when death comes calling."

I nod in agreement and resolve to covertly help anyone who comes to me from those homes.

Permission to go to the grove and the woods surrounding it means I will see him. My heart leaps at the thought. Surely, I imagined the tender storm in his eyes, and his intensity. One does not bare who they truly are upon first meeting.

All my life I have been warned against the pull of the tide and the strange creatures who rule there. My mother's gaze was far away when she told me to guard my heart against them. Against the one who would break the covenant.

When I carried her limp body across the threshold, I remembered her last warning. As the ribbons of blood snaked across the blanket of leaves she told me I was meant for naught but chaos and tragedy. As she stripped the crystal from around her neck and placed it around mine, she said my hard-headed, foolish ways would lead me into the arms of my enemy. A saltwater prince.

I've sensed her here, watching me. Her spirit eyes are full of sorrow when she tries to convey her message. The words are indiscernible, as if she's speaking through water. The only one I can ever make out is "Beware."

When I crossed the threshold with her wheezing form in my arms and laid her down by the hearth, my stepfather collapsed over her body and sobbed like a broken man. When he put away his sorrow and turned to me with a red-rimmed, accusatory glare, the rod became the language he spoke.

He blames me for her death. When he has drunk enough ale to fell a dragon he says if I hadn't sought the company of trees and wild things, of things forbidden, she would be alive. I resent his condemnation but know there is a kernel of truth in his bitter complaints. I was certain my power would be enough to control whatever it called down. My certainty was born of youthful rebellion and petulance because I wanted to prove my readiness to my mother. I'd just turned fifteen and she denied me my heart's desire.

She was right to deny me. She'd claimed I wasn't a diligent enough student to dance in the grove at Bealtaine. According to her, my demonstration of maturity and sound judgment was lacking and I would be denied access to the festival mysteries until I displayed more discipline.

I'd been furious and decided to dance around the ring of stones within the grove at the height of the new moon alone. It is the only time calling on the crone and her denizens lifts a veil between the worlds.

My ignorance raised a vengeful ancient power instead. My mother spilt her blood to protect me from the eldritch Forest Lord. My recklessness garnered his attention, and she made the sacrifice to banish him and ensure my safety. I bear the guilt of her death.

As I scrub the bowls and sweep the day's grit of dust from the stone floor, I wonder if my mother was right in all things. If I meet Eachann Lir in the grove tomorrow, will chaos and tragedy ensue? Will the gods and goddesses finally force me to pay for my ignorance?

The singing in my veins is too much a part of me to ignore. My heart does not care if he is finally the thing that breaks us. My heart does not care if his caress will paint the world red with blood or leave destruction in its wake.

When I finally lay down on my pallet in front of the hearth, the dying embers morph into my dreams. I remember the way my body trembled when he leaned over the casement. How my heart caught in my throat at his covetous gaze and provocative words. When I dream, I see him limned in fading light, a golden, gleaming prince with the cold might of the sea in his eyes. He is covered in runes I want to trace with my fingertips, and there are lines of laughter that trek from the corners of his eyes. I want to feel that laughter rumble against my skin.

Chapter Six

Eachann

The creeping close of the forest on every side sends a shiver down the base of my spine. Our islands are scoured by wind and sea, and my kind come ashore on white sand where we have clear sight and a clean sweep of our sword if need be. The presence of so many trees clustered together makes my beast skitter and snort his discomfort.

I know the grove of birch and rowan is her sanctuary, so I am determined to set aside my foreboding.

When she glides around the bend, the gleam of evening sun on her hair sets it afire. Until she is nothing but a golden flame. She's singing, a tralala story of a lovelorn sailor and his selkie wife. The way the selkie is portrayed in the bard's tale amuses me. Every selkie I've ever known is sullen and enigmatic. Being sweet and accommodating is foreign to them. If I hadn't found my witch, what sort of marriage would have bound me? I cannot go through with the betrothal my father has arranged. Any doubts I had about the wisdom of pursuing this woman now seem inconsequential.

"A selkie would not stay ashore for so long."

My observation startles her, and her trilling comes to an abrupt halt when I emerge from the shelter of the trees. She hurtles toward me, grinning and eager. I catch her in my arms as if I have always known her particular momentum and weight. As if she belongs there and nowhere else. I lay my cheek against the crown of her head as I twirl her around.

Her hands bracket my cheeks, and her eyes are twinkling deep green. Like the dappled shadows that shimmer across the surface of the sea.

"What do you have against selkies?"

I brush a dewy strand of hair from her forehead and tuck it behind her ear. "I know they are feckless creatures. Never content. That is how I know a selkie bride would never stay."

Her eyes search mine. "But what of true love? In all the pain and horror of the world, what if they found that Elysia together? Something beautiful to build between them from that which is broken? A place to lay down their burdens?"

Her winsome smile is earnest.

"You speak of more than the loyalty of selkies."

She shrugs. "Aye. You may think it is a silly song, and an inaccurate portrayal of the truth. But I see it as a tale of what we do for love. The sacrifice we must make when we choose to follow where it leads. It is not about the selkie bride or her regrets and reluctance. It is about the actions that led to her regret. The power of feeling that once overcame what seemed like insurmountable obstacles."

I set her on the ground and step away. Her expression is solemn now. As if those intriguing dimples weren't creasing her cheeks a moment ago.

"You have had time to consider the wisdom of this alliance between us."

She raises a brow. "Is that what you've decided to name it? A mere alliance? It is far more than that. A precarious bargain between enemies. A dance straight into the heart of a bonfire. Two people setting aside centuries of hatred because their souls hold the same shadows. An act of defiance and rebellion neither one of them fully understands."

"I understand it."

"Then explain it to me. Because I do not. I tossed and turned on my cold pallet last night. I watched the logs in the hearth turn to ash because I could not lay my thoughts to rest and the sea-salt scent of you lingered on my skin even though we barely touched. I imagined the world burning to ash all around us."

I want to step forward again, but she is wary. Like one of the red does that prances daintily into the froth of the morning tide. "I tossed and turned as well. My brother already warned me against you. Against pursuing anything more between us. He repeatedly reminded me that meeting you here was impetuous, idiotic and dangerous. I have been impetuous before and it is only his warrior instinct that saved me from disaster. He waits just over the rise." I point in the direction of the hill behind me.

"I have no one to speak with about my reservations. No one to hear my confession of fear and doubt. If my stepfather and stepbrothers were to follow me here, they would chase you back to your kingdom with howling hounds and cold steel. You have your brother to act as your conscience and question the wisdom of your actions. To do so while still offering his protection."

"I ask what is this more than an alliance to be? Shall I become both lover and confessor? I cannot assign you acts of penitence. There is no sin or reproach in this. You need not fear me or my kind. I have told you I will shed my own blood before endangering you."

"If a tryst on the edge of a forest, where you are helpless to call down your magic, ends in your destruction, there will be sin in this. My sin."

"You are full of contradictions. How can you celebrate the love between a selkie and a fisherman and toss and turn on your pallet when you think of us?"

"That is just a bard's tale. What we are embarking on is at odds with all we have learned. My dreams were full of fire and destruction. I have been its instrument before and my selfishness destroyed one I loved. I should tread carefully instead of running to meet you."

If she denies what is between us, I will lose control of my beast. He will break free and rend and reap until she is ours. In death or in life. "You have been chosen as my mate."

"So you claim. I feel the pull of that destiny as well, but do not know what it means. Not truly. The intensity of it frightens me. Like I shall perish if you are not in this world. You haunted my dreams last night."

I reach for her hands again, and this time she does not retreat. "It means that I will carry you to my kingdom upon my back. It means you will bear my sons. It means that I am wholly yours and you are wholly mine. That I will honor and protect you with my lifespan. Whether it be five hundred years or ten thousand."

"Five hundred years is unfathomable. Ten thousand years even more unfathomable than that."

"An each uisge's lifespan is always uncertain. It is hard to kill us, but not impossible. And ofttimes, the Old Ones simply decide it is our time, and the sea claims us so what we are becomes nothing more than coral and froth and weathered stone."

"Five hundred years is far beyond a mortal lifespan. Even for those of us with witchery in our veins."

"When an each uisge mate accepts the sigils of the ceremony, she is imbued with the strength and immortality of the creature she has accepted into her heart. If you agree to let me claim you, my long life becomes yours as well."

She raises a brow. "So you would carry me to this kingdom and I would bear your children. What more is there to this life? Would I be no more than a vessel for your seed?"

"The women of our kingdom are far more than vessels. You would have the freedom and independence to pursue your magic and healing. You would have the resources of our library at your fingertips. A repository grander than that once housed in Alexandria."

"I have spent my entire life in this simple village. My learning in all but magic is rudimentary. I will not be able to read any of those ancient tomes."

"I will teach you."

"Yet another vow. My heart wants to believe them, but my thoughts are full of doubt. This may be destiny, and the hand of magic or gods, but it is swift and sudden. I feel perilously close to drowning."

"It is swift and sudden. But it is not drowning. It is soaring. My soul has wings, like an albatross who has flown across the world, seeking its rest. There is contentedness and awe here..." I thump my knuckles against my heart. "Because the rest I have been seeking is in sight."

"I've known little peace in my life – you are certes you find your own in me?"

I brush my knuckles across her cheek. It is a pale imitation of the way I want to curl her into my body, but she rests her chin in my palm. "Aye. I am certain. More certain than I am of the tides, or my sister's tendency to lecture us about ancient tales over the evening meal, or of my brother Callum's affinity for the sword."

"This will not be easy."

"Nothing worth having is easy, mo chridhe fiadhaich."

"And you will have me?"

I don't bother hiding my need for her. "Aye, leannan. I will have you. I will be patient until I do."

"You will have need of it."

I know the men in her life have never shown her kindness. I know she is more like the red doe than she knows – easily spooked and resistant to taming. But I will lure her with kisses of honey and words of praise. Not because my beast wants to carry her on its back and disappear beneath the waves, but because she quiets the sharp scythe of his ferocity.

I raise her hand to my lips and kiss each knuckle. "Go. Before I steal more than you are ready to give. I must depart as well. If not, there will be more than imaginary arrows in my shoulders borne of my brother's exasperation."

She steps away and gathers her basket. "Farewell, Prince of the Sea."

I watch her until she's no more than a flicker of bright hair.

Callum claps me on the shoulder, shaking his head. "Come along, Besotted One."

Chapter Seven

Galanta

The basket on my arm is full of the day's harvest.
There has been someone at the door of our cottage
all hours of the night because the fever is rampant now.
The thatcher's children are barely clinging to this world

and the young lad whose mother begged my assistance slipped away this very morning. I found enough to replenish my depleted stores and I think I've found a way to combat the sickness decimating the village one household at a time. If I'm permitted to treat them. Two of the fishermen made the sign of the evil eye in my direction as I walked past their cottages last evening and I think the cronies of the priest have been sowing his venom.

He called me mo chridhe fiadhaich. His wild heart. I cannot let myself be wild in this place. I must be subdued and conscious of my duty to heal. I must ignore the call of the crystal around my neck. I must ignore the wards cast against me when I pass.

I should be full of purpose because I've been using my skill as my mother intended me to. For the good of my fellow villagers. I should be content because any opportunity to administer care to others is a way to make up for my rash youth. But I am also filled with fear. Public opinion can be easily swayed to cast me as the villain. Especially if the priest has his say.

He's become more attentive to my comings and goings of late, and I know I should exercise more caution. But the thought of stepping into the shadows of the forest, hearing the leaves sing in the breeze, and finding him there waiting makes my heart light and my stride fleet.

I set the basket on the floor by the hearth and gather what I'll need to prepare the evening meal. I'm kneading the maslin for a loaf of bread, when there's a knock at the back door. I swipe my hands over my apron and swing it open.

I'm shocked to see the tavern maid is standing there. She has never had a reason to seek me out. I've always believed it's because she knows she and my stepbrothers have an uncommon arrangement and she doesn't want to impose or cause me embarrassment. I cannot interpret her expression, so I pull her through the door. I am disobeying my stepfather's command, but she is far too conspicuous standing in the open doorway. I hope she escaped the notice of anyone who will carry tales to the forge. Especially the priest and his minions.

"Why have you sought me out?"

She sighs heavily and swallows. "I am with child."

Her confession is angry.

"You'll want herbs to strengthen your blood for the babe's health."

She laughs harshly and hooks my arms with a desperate expression. "Herbs to strengthen my blood are not the reason I have sought you out."

"What other reason could you possibly have?"

She scowls. "I do not want this babe. It is likely the seed of one of your miserable stepbrothers. They are churlish, and fight over me like dogs contesting a bone. But when we are all in accord, the arrangement we have suits me fine. I do not wish to disrupt it. I have no desire to be a mother."

"I do not use my knowledge for harm."

"Argh! There is no harm in this. The babe isn't even a babe. My courses are only a handspan late, and my breasts are not yet tender. But I know the signs."

"You have no children."

She smirks. "Precisely. Your mother gave me pennyroyal the last time and my difficulty was resolved."

"My mother gave it to you?" I cannot believe my mother set aside her own rules.

"Aye. She did. She claimed that as a servant of the Goddess, she had to abide by the wishes of those who would, or would not, be mothers. She said all things have a season, and if I did not feel this was my one for bearing a child, she would not force it upon me."

I do not sense a lie in her confession. My mother never spoke of this side of her craft, and this is the first time one of the women has requested such a thing of me. I have the knowledge and the ingredients on hand, but I do not wish to rouse the dark power trapped within the crystal. Or come to the notice of the priest. He complains that midwifery gives women too much power over life and death. Dispensing this remedy will be far more insidious than midwifery.

"Meet me at the edge of the grove just after dawn. They'll have left for the forge by then."

Her face breaks into a grin and she dips her head in gratitude. "I knew you would help me. And your brothers need never know."

As she slips away, I ponder what this will mean. I already hold so many secrets, and now I must hold one more. One of my stepbrothers would beat me for if it was unearthed. The pulse of the crystal beneath my chemise is like a warning. As if it senses the balance of things will soon be upset.

I left word at the forge that I would return at dusk. I have spent the day here after delivering the physick to my patient.

My prince is waiting at the edge of the glade. His back is to me, the crossed swords a potent reminder of who and what he is. The tender storm I saw in his eyes is not the only storm he is capable of. There are stories of the ways his people have called down the sea and destroyed entire villages when they have felt slighted or betrayed.

My footfalls startle him from his reverie, and he whirls around, his hand on the pommel of the sword strapped to his side.

His face breaks into a wide smile when he recognizes me. "My green girl."

I run and hurl myself into his arms as he strides toward me.

When I bury my face in his neck, he lifts me up, and I let the salt brine scent of him seep into me.

His power is muted here because he is far from the sea. He is making himself vulnerable to attack. But every evening at dusk, this is where I find him. Waiting for me. Every meeting, we grow more impatient, our kisses escalating and essential. As necessary as the breaths we take.

I lower my head so I can brush my lips with his. So I can feel his laughter.

Because he's laughing at my eagerness and his own. At this impossible connection we're helpless to deny.

"All day long, foraging in the underbrush, you filled my thoughts."

"And all day long, at sword practice and seated on my throne, you filled my thoughts."

He raises a finger to the thin streak of blood on his cheek.

"Callum managed to catch me off guard because I was distracted by the thought of your lips and imagining the feel of you in my arms. The supplicants who petitioned the court today were confused by my answers to their queries. Because my mind was elsewhere."

I glide my lips over the scarlet thread. "We're quite the pair. Two lovelorn enemies."

"You are not my enemy. You are my salvation."

The kiss he presses to the crown of my head tempts me to close my eyes in surrender.

I feel safe and warm in his embrace. Like no harm shall ever come again. Like every mistake was a step in the right direction.

I reluctantly step away and crouch to set the basket on the ground. "I cannot stay long. I left word I would return at dusk. I have been gone all day due to the disconcerting supplicant who begged my assistance last night. I snatched a handful of berries, but my stomach growls in protest at the lack of sustenance."

"I have a flask of wine and a hunk of cheese. You will eat and tell me of your mysterious visitor. Let us make the most of the time we have."

"Is eating your food like eating offerings from fairies? Will I be locked in a dance I cannot escape?"

"You should ken by now that you will never escape me, leannan. So sit upon yon rock and I will feed you."

"So long as I am home by dusk." I clamber onto the flat rock and arrange the folds of my kirtle. "I shouldn't tell you of my visitor – it is not my place to share another's secrets."

"This visitor disconcerted you for a reason, and I would know it. Whatever secret they shared weighs heavy across your brow. I can almost see it glimmering there."

We have only known one another a handful of weeks, but I feel as if I have known him all my days. I need to unburden this secret to someone - or it will press down upon me in my dreams. "A woman came to me today because she did not want the babe she's carrying."

"Babes are not always convenient. It is not uncommon. Why was this disconcerting? Surely, you've been approached before as the only cunning woman in your village?"

I shake my head. "I've never been approached. But this woman claimed she sought my mother's assistance another time and my mother granted it without quarrel." I cast my gaze downward and rub the knob of the crystal beneath my gown.

He's there in two swift strides, tilting my chin up, his gaze fierce. "Our parents keep their own counsel for reasons we do not always understand. I know my father is so focused on the welfare of his kingdom, ofttimes he is too busy to see to the welfare of his family. You should not dwell on this part of her that seems to contradict what you knew of her nature. Instead, you should do as your heart and your conscience tell you to do."

"I met her here this morning and gave her the purgative with instructions on how to administer it."

"Do you fear she will betray you?"

"No," I scoff. "She's not at all eager to bear the child of one of my stepbrothers."

"Your stepbrothers are not good men?"

"They are boors who think women are nothing more than a place to stick their cocks."

"That is often how your kind think of women. There are some each uisge who believe it as well." He smiles wryly as he sits on the ground and leans his back against one of the towering trees.

I lower myself until I'm sitting beside him. "That was your philosophy at one time?"

"When I was a stripling, yes. All I dreamt of was all the places I wanted to stick my cock. Some men, some women."

"Your lack of discernment is not attractive."

He shrugs. "It was also over a thousand years ago. Before I learned to practice discernment. Before my mother thumped the side of my head so frequently she drilled it into my skull that every single creature deserves respect and consideration and was not created solely for my enjoyment."

"The sheer arrogance."

He blushes. "I cannot deny the truth. I'm still arrogant in many ways. But not in that way."

He hands me the wine flask, and when I tip it back, his gaze fastens on the movement of my throat.

"You are watching me very intently."

"Just imagining the way your throat will move in other ways."

I raise my brow. "I've heard the rowdy talk of my stepbrothers when they've consumed too much ale. I know what you're referring to."

"I cannot help my runaway thoughts. You consume them. And me."

I giggle mischievously. "You want me to consume you."

His mouth curves in an answering grin and he shouts with laughter before his eyes fill with heat. "Aye, I do. More than anything."

"Convincing me will require more than a few stolen moments, a flask of wine and a hunk of cheese."

His eyes crease again in laughter. "I am well aware how difficult you will be to convince, mo chridhe fiadhaich."

"Though you're loathe to admit it, mo stoirm, I believe there have been very few times in your life that required you to earn your reward."

"Earn my reward? You call me a storm. What makes you think I don't claim what I think should be my reward whether I've earned it or not?"

I shake my head. "I know you don't. You're arrogant. But not about things that matter so deeply. You would never press your suit where it was not wanted. Whether or not you wanted it."

"Is my suit unwanted?"

"You know it is not. And you know your method of convincing me will eventually win me over."

"And how do I know this?"

"Because I am here. With you. Drinking wine and flirting against my better judgment."

"Finish your wine. And put the cheese in your satchel for later."

"Why?"

"Because I need to kiss you, and our time is nearly up. I'd not miss an opportunity to convince."

He beckons me near and gathers me to him again. His kiss lands softly on the upturned corner of my grin. I grin wider and burrow my hands into the loose sunlight of his hair. Most of its escaped from the thong he used to tie it back, and I use my grip to haul him closer. Our breaths mingle as one and our limbs tangle like a fisherman's knot.

His laughter is a gentle rumble against my lips as he nuzzles my cheek. "If I'd had the foresight to strap a blanket beneath my swords; I could have laid you down in this grove and let the wind rattle about us and the snow drift at will."

He groans into my ear, and I share his torture. I can feel the solid length of him against my thigh. Even through the barrier of woolen hose and belted kirtle and muffled cloak.

"I would follow you anywhere if I could." I murmur. This is madness, this wanting on such short acquaintance. It is more than lust or greed.

Every evening the hour we have with each other seems shorter and less. He is nothing like the fearsome stories that paint him as a villainous, evil creature who seeks to drown our kind and leave our bones to molder beneath the tides.

"I want to take you with me to the keep. You would be safe there from this." His eyes darken as he rubs his thumb across the scar on my upper cheek.

"It is little enough sacrifice to ensure those who are the weakest among us have a chance for survival."

"This was your reward for trying to ease the pain and suffering of others?"

It's not my reward, it's the penance I've imposed on myself as punishment for my past arrogance and foolhardiness. "The rancor of my stepfather is a small price to pay."

"Mo chridhe fiadhiach," he whispers against the crown of my head as he snugs me against him.

This is what he calls me. Wild heart. His wild heart. "Mo stoirm."

He is my storm and so much more. These moments that dwindle too quickly between us are barely enough to sustain me against the crushing weight of the world that buffets me about.

"My father is pressuring me to wed one of the selkie princesses."

"A fickle selkie?"

He laughs at my teasing tone. "Aye, a fickle selkie."

"You have not told him of us." I haven't mentioned him either.

"Callum is the only one who knows why I've come ashore so frequently the last few weeks. Even now, he stands guard just beyond that rise."

"He will not betray us?"

Eachann sighs. "Nay. Even though he thinks me a fool, he'll not betray us."

"Why is this thing between us forbidden?"

"I only know half the story. A witch of your kind slew one of our kings when he came ashore to retrieve the bride he'd been promised. Our army destroyed the village in retaliation, wiping all memory of it to the depths of the sea."

"And yet we rebuilt."

His mouth quirks into a grin. "Aye. Mortals are tenacious. It's quite galling at times."

"And your kind are not tenacious or galling?"

"We likely are. I'll let you be the judge of that, leanann."

Chapter Eight

Eachann

She will soon learn that I am just as tenacious as she is.
I want to know every facet of her. The full story
of how she came to practice her herbal craft in secret, and

weave spells into everything she touches. The whole truth of the skeins that cross her loom and what she chants over them as she weaves. How she finds the strength to meet the gaze of those who persecute her without backing down. How she bears the pain and where she goes inside her head when the bough breaks across her back. She is tenacious. But so am I.

"How did you come by these scars?" I raise her hand and crest my lips over the faded welts.

She won't confirm my suspicions, but she doesn't need to. I know the answer to my question. How dare that sanctimonious bastard lay a hand on her? How long has she borne it? Why does her family allow it to happen?

"I bear them willingly."

She speaks of her mother's death. She was a mere child – a stripling, but still a child. She may have been headstrong, but however her mother died, she is not to blame. "You should not. You have made amends for whatever despicable deeds you believe you committed. You have done nothing that warrants continued persecution. They should be ashamed."

"Until you, I had no hope of escape. I had no choice other than accepting whatever punishment they meted out."

She has borne too much for one so young. I tilt her face toward mine and lower my mouth to give her comfort and remind her I will stand for her now. She stretches and meets me halfway.

The first touch of her lips is like rough silk against my own. I can feel the indentations on her bottom lip where she has bitten it. Either in fear or concentration or to soothe her nerves. I let my own lips rest there, wanting to absorb even that little prick of pain. I feel the fragility of her in my arms and I want to scoop her up and run toward the waves.

Her mouth is soft and sweet. She tastes of wild mint and the red berries she harvests from the bramble at the edge of the forest. Her lips are stained from the tart juice and I smile because she can never resist snatching a handful on her way here. She rests one hand against my chest and I press into it, so I can feel her touch like a brand, scorching through skin and bone to the heart of the beast clamoring inside me.

The corner of her mouth dips into the enticing curl of a dimple when I nip it. It becomes even deeper, a slash accentuating her cheek when I push aside the neckline of her kirtle. Her shoulder is dusted with golden freckles, and I want to trace constellations over them with my tongue.

I plant a single kiss along her jaw and caress her nape with the palm of my hand. She mewls like a forlorn kitten and arches closer. When I meet her gaze, I can see her impatience. She purses her lips and winds her grip into the folds of my mantle.

"Is that all you're going to show me, sea prince?"

I growl into her ear. "It's all I trust myself to give you right now, green girl."

I grasp her hand and move it over my trews. So she can feel how desperate I am for every piece of her.

"You are eager for me." She observes with a smug grin.

"Feeling accomplished, are we?"

"Well, by your own confession, you have lived at least a thousand years. Which means you have far more experience than I and have lain with hundreds, if not thousands, of lovers. And I have moved you to desperation."

I cannot tamp down the rough confession that rises to my lips. "Lass, I have never felt this way. And it's not about the chase. I want to cage you against one of these trees and drop to my knees, so I can taste your arousal. I want to feel my cock in the snug clasp of your fist. I want to anoint every inch of your soft skin with my tongue and teeth."

Her hand trembles over me and her cheeks darken in a blush that rivals the fiery tresses that trail over her shoulders. It suffuses her face, and blends into her hairline. The breath feathering across my throat becomes a ragged staccato and those leaf-green eyes flicker with hunger. "I wish we could stop time. I wish my family could fend for themselves on the loaf of oat bread I left cooling on the table and a piece of salted pork. I wish we had the whole day together, so you could do all those things instead of these stolen moments we carve out and hoard."

"And I wish my irksome brother wasn't glaring daggers into my back and silently counting backward and forward because he thinks I've tarried too long. The weight of his silent judgment is something I'll gladly bear in exchange for our first kiss."

She lifts the back of her hand to her lips. "You have my gratitude for making my first kiss memorable. I shall cherish it."

My brows lower. "We will exchange many more kisses, mo chridhe fiadhaich."

"Brother, if ye dinnae wish to be stranded by the tide, ye need to take your leave of yer paramour."

Knowing he's right doesn't make me resent his interruption any less.

Callum is loyal to a fault, and that is why he accompanies me every night. But he doesn't understand my fascination. Or why I so recklessly risk discovery. I cannot wait to see him catapult head over heels for the woman fated to be his. I will tease him as mercilessly as he has scoffed at me.

"I do not trust myself to kiss you again, leannan. I will hold you past darkness and I would loathe myself if you suffered because of it."

She strides forward, grabs my face, and pecks me on the tip of my nose and the bow of my mouth before stepping away. "I will see you tomorrow, mo stoirm." The farewell trails over her shoulder as she glides away.

I watch until she's a mere glimmer of shining hair dancing through the leaves. The words of the selkie song slip along the breeze and coax me into a smile.

"Ye're a lovesick fool, brother."

"No, Callum, I am not. This is not a sickness. It is living for the first time in thousands of years. Gods willing, someday you will understand what it is to hold such awe in your heart."

I make a vow to myself. That I will protect her and avenge her against all harm. Past, present and future.

I will speak to Callum on the morrow. And our wily aunt. She has deftly orchestrated the rise and fall of many a mortal kingdom. Extricating her from her situation will require strategy and tactical maneuvering.

"I understand why you wish to intervene, but we should not involve ourselves in village politics."

My brother and wily great-aunt Arianrhod take the midday meal with me in the antechamber.

Callum is confident he's being the voice of reason. But there is no reason in this. "It's not politics. It's brutality. He's preying on those who are weaker instead of protecting them."

My aunt taps her cane upon the stone floor. "If you threaten him, she will suffer all the more."

"Not if he fears my retaliation."

Callum shakes his head. "I think you're making a mistake. Is anyone in her village aware of your connection?"

"Nay, not yet."

"You are foolish, boy. If you threaten the priest, your relationship will become public knowledge. She may no longer have the freedom to meet you." The tap of her cane against the stone is rapid, betraying her disquiet.

"But she'll be safe."

Both wear expressions of disbelief.

"At least there will be no more scars on her wrists."

"Brother, you cannot think to kidnap her and suffer no consequences. What if you are liberating her from one circumstance to only bring her to a new hell? She is not your consecrated mate and does not bear your sigil."

"And what of the alliance your parents seek? It is one designed to protect our kingdom."

"I see no reason why she cannot bear my sigil. That's easily remedied. And surely my father will devise another means of pacifying the selkie queen."

"You speak from ignorance, nephew. Your father is insistent you wed the princess for reasons you do not understand. It is more than a political alliance. More than the move of armies across a chessboard. He won't be happy you've kept this from him."

"When it becomes necessary, I'll deal with his displeasure and explain myself. If I decide to bring her here, will you help me?"

"Why do you seek my help?" My aunt's tone is sharp.

"You are known for your cunning, Aunt. For the tact and finesse you bring to the most delicate of situations."

"So, I am to help you make this betrayal of your father's trust seem palatable."

Her tone is caustic.

"You'll always have the promise of my sword." Callum assures me. "Even if I think your schemes are harebrained."

I nod in appreciation and clap him on the shoulder. I feel their gazes on me as I leave and know I have gained their reluctant support.

Chapter Nine

Galanta

My stepbrothers were in a foul mood last night. When I asked Fergus what ailed them, he snarled at me to leave them to their ale and launched his wooden spoon at my head. Luckily his aim was terrible because of the ale.

Dougal was the one to alleviate my curiosity. When he told me that Rhona was lying abed, dread suffused me and skated down my spine. If she perishes, Fergus and Dougal will be on a rampage to ferret out the cause. If my part in her affliction comes to light, I'll have no control over my brothers or the repercussions of my actions. I pray to the goddess her indisposition wasn't caused by the pennyroyal infusion. If she was careless of the directions I gave, and took the entire infusion in one sitting, she's ill indeed. It may be the death of her.

She has her own secrets to keep. But that does not mean I am safe from revelation if she slips into feverish dreams. I bury my worry because I do not want it to spoil my time with my prince. He is the brightest part of my life, and I will hold onto that feeling as long as I can.

When I step into our hidden meeting place, he's pulling a flask of wine and some cheese from the satchel slung over his shoulder.

"Are you bribing me, prince?"

The grin he launches in my direction makes my heart catapult.

"You're as slender as one of the reeds at the edge of the shore. I'm not bribing you; I'm making certain the wind doesn't carry you away before I can."

I slide my hand beneath the collar of his tunic. While he's distracted by the stroke of my fingers over his runes, I slip the wine from his grasp and hold the flask aloft. "So this is an investment?"

"Among other things."

I lower myself to recline against the tree and cross my arms. "I want to know what those other things are."

He drops to the ground and leans back against his own tree, mirroring my pose. "Not a bribe, exactly. But certainly a way to entice you. Something to erase your resolve. A way to loosen your tongue and tell me why you seem so brittle this evening."

He is far too perceptive. Or he's the first person ever to pay such close attention to me. "I do not want to cloud our time together with my troubles."

"If they are your troubles, they are my troubles. Although I have yet to fully convince you of it, I am your mate."

"The woman I helped lies abed."

He can't hide his alarm. "Is it mere coincidence?"

I shrug and take another swig of wine. "I don't know. I cannot ask her. What if she decided to take the entire infusion at once?"

"Did you not instruct her on the proper use?"

"Yes. But ofttimes those who come to me think taking the entire concoction is a swifter remedy. In most cases their ignorance causes nothing more than an upset stomach. But if she took the entire infusion of pennyroyal, it could affect her heart, or cause her to fall into an unawakenable sleep."

"If she falls into such a sleep, she will spread no tales."

Because I have reached the same conclusion, I cannot chastise him for his dark observation. "I can only pray to the goddess that if coming to my door caused her malady my involvement remains a secret."

"What will happen if it becomes known you gave her the means to end her pregnancy?"

"The priest has made it known far and wide he believes women have no place in healing or midwifery and a woman's lot is to bear children. Whether the mother lives or dies."

"Then you must do all you can to ensure your part in this is not uncovered."

"Even more so because she is the leman of my brothers." He looks astonished at this. "They openly share her?"

"It's not that simple. In our culture, before the advent of the church, it was not uncommon for a woman to take as many lovers as she pleased. There was no shame in it. Just as there was no shame in men loving one another. It is only with the establishment of the church that the women of these islands lost that freedom."

"I have been the object of sharing in the past, and I have shared my lovers. When you live a long life, there are few positions or arrangements you have not been a part of."

Now I am astonished. "There is no shame for these things in your culture?"

"If the parties are unmated, there is no shame. If one of them is mated, there are consequences."

"Such as?"

He grimaces. "Our friend Carrig's mother was murdered by her mate when he found out she carried the son of the Kraken King instead of his seed."

"I fear that will be my fate as well if I am found out. Likely at the hand of my stepbrothers."

"How often must I assure you that I will let no harm befall you? Not one hair on your head shall be severed, nor one inch of your skin marked?"

I shake my head. "Though I have not felt the rod on my back since our meeting, so long as I remain here, I will never completely escape the threat of it. The priest watches me with the eyes of an eagle, waiting for any hint of infraction. I'd be made to suffer at least ten lashes and months in the cell beneath his church if it became known I keep frequent company with a creature he believes is an abomination in the eyes of his god."

"How will you ensure the maid keeps your secret?"

"I will check on her tomorrow, under the auspices of charity, and hope my ruse is believed."

"If aught goes awry, you will get word to me via one of the ravens."

"One of the ravens?"

"They are the messengers of your goddess, and you are one of her chosen. They will gladly carry any message you give them."

"Is that why they follow me about?"

"Yes. And they are an offer of protection. If your goddess is anything like Lir, she does all she can to protect her devotees."

"Her power wanes. I fear it will not be enough to save me if salvation is required."

"If your devotion is not enough, find a way to send word."

"A part of me believes I deserve whatever fate I am dealt."

"You have darkness in you. Otherwise my beast would not be so compelled to claim you. But you have light as well. You truly want to use your skills for the good of others."

"You do not know what I am capable of."

"The great evils you believe you have committed cannot compare to what I have done to protect my kingdom. But please, share your secrets so I may absolve you."

I rest my head on my knees and swivel it in his direction. "You cannot absolve me. Not of these deeds. These woods hold dark magic."

"Like that of the sea? My kingdom is full of darkness as well."

I tangle my hands together and stare at them. "When I was a petulant child, I lured the eldritch god from his lair. My mother died to protect me. Here, inside this grove, she gave her blood to save me."

"She chose to give her life for you. Her choice is not your burden to bear."

"If I'd heeded her words, there would have been no choice."

"Why are you so convinced of your guilt? You were a child."

"A child who should have known better. My life was steeped in dangerous tales of those of my kind who called to creatures beyond the green veil."

"As children we are most drawn to that which is forbidden. Even as grown men and women it is hard for us to resist temptation."

"If only my ignorance was so easily excused."

"We are warned as well. Of caves too near the ocean floor and what terrors they hold. Of gods from the deep who will wrench the soul of our beast from us – so we are only rage and madness."

"And like an obedient child, you paid heed to those warnings. I did not."

He shrugs. "I was curious, but not curious enough."

"It wasn't just curiosity. I was rebellious. I was under the mistaken impression I would have more control over the summoning than my mother. Than my grandmother."

"The old gods are full of trickery. You couldn't have known your rebellion would equal her death."

"They demand a sacrifice for every summoning. My mother's warning echoed in my ears from infancy. And still I thought I was above it. That I could control the outcome. When he emerged from the rowan grove, he had a crown of thorns on his brow. And his arrows aimed at me. My mother darted ahead. She grabbed one of his arrows and let the sharp edge of it scrape her palm."

"She turned it toward him?"

"No, she turned it on herself. She used it to slice her wrists, muttering incantations about blood sacrifice. It was a bargain I did not understand. The eldritch king's face was twisted in fury, because whatever old lore she used banished him once again."

"That is why the priest fears you. Because the legacy of that power flows in your veins. It is perchance what drew my beast as well. You follow the old ways."

"I do so in secret. A profession of my true devotion would end in calamity. My flesh crackling in fire as I am burned at the stake. That fate would have befallen me before now if anyone truly knew what happened in this grove those long years ago."

"You have never recounted the events to anyone?"

"You are the first to hear the truth of what happened."

"Why am I now the keeper of your secrets?"

"Something compels me to give them to you. All of them. Because I know you will keep them, and me, safe from harm. My mind tells me I should not give my trust so easily, but my heart gallops forward without reservation."

"My younger brother Callum has always been the keeper of my secrets. But now I am compelled to give them to you. Someday, when we have time within our grasp that is not stolen, I will tell you my whole story, mo chridhe fiadhaich. And hope you do not flee in terror."

"Just as your beast recognizes the darkness in me and is drawn to it, so am I drawn to you, mo stoirm. Because you are chaos and fury. But you are also passion, courage, and tenderness. You have shown me all these things with your words. I am certain a recounting of your deeds would show them as well."

"Each parting from you is sorrow heaped on sorrow. I am the most alive I have ever been in these moments with you."

"I feel the same. But I cannot allow my feelings to sway me before it is time."

"I will wait until there is white in your hair and your hands are gnarled with age, mo chridhe."

"I will not be permitted to live a long life here. That is what my dreams foretell. But I am compelled to do all I can to heal before even that privilege is taken from me."

"Go. Take leave of me before I can no longer bear the thought of it and keep you here against your will."

I set the flask down and rise to my feet. Just as I do every evening, I clasp his face and bring it down to me for a brief, smacking kiss.

"Tomorrow is Bealtaine. Meet me on the edge of the bonfires."

I can feel his gaze burning into my back as I whirl away.

I sought out Rhona's cottage today. It is squat and dark and hovers in the shadow of the tavern where she spends her days and nights.

I want to know how she came to this life, but it is not my place to ask. The warped oak door swings open at my soft rap.

A grizzled woman in a grease-stained apron fists her hands on her hips and looks me up and down with a sneer. "I know who you are. We have no need of your kind."

She's blocking me from entering, but the room is filled with quiet moaning. "I can help her."

"Curse her, more like. We don't need your help, witch."

She grins at my sharp intake of breath. "Never been called that to your face?"

I haven't. I thought at least some of the villagers were grateful for my presence. "No. Because I am not one."

"Not according to the church. You use your herbs to meddle. That makes you a witch."

My healing is the least witchy part of my nature. But I will never share the rest with anyone in this village. "I just want to help her," I repeat.

"There's aught you can do. She's feverish now, and her belly roils."

"Then this is the time she needs me most." I press determinedly forward, but the woman is a stone wall.

"I'm not letting you cross this threshold, no matter how much you plead and toss your pretty head. I am not a fool."

"The next few hours are crucial. If we do not break her fever, she will perish."

"If she perishes, it will be the will of God."

"You are making a grave mistake."

Her expression hardens. "You'll not curse this household. Begone, witch." She shoves me backward and the door crashes shut in the wake of her banishment.

My hands are shaking when I pull the hood of my cloak up to shield my face. I do not think my brothers' leman will live through the night. I came here because it is my fault she is in this state, on the verge of death. I should have refused her when she demanded the remedy. I fear my attempt to alleviate her pain will make my own situation worse.

Chapter Ten

Galanta

The celebration has been underway since the moon rose. It waxes full and casts a pale glamor over everything it touches. The ale and wine have flowed copiously, and those who chose to honor the old ways this night and welcome the change of season are well past caring how one lone girl spends her time. Or who she spends it with. Those who follow the edicts of the priest and have forsaken the grove are snug in their beds with crosses beneath their pillows. Though my stepfather and stepbrothers claim they follow the new religion, they were bleary-eyed and well into their cups tonight. It was ridiculously easy for me to sneak away.

My encounter earlier today unnerved me. My thoughts have been muddled and I didn't exercise caution around my family. My stepfather cuffed my cheek when I stumbled over my stepbrother's feet and spilt soup down the front of his tunic. Fergus and Dougal derive sadistic amusement from impeding my progress through the cottage. And anytime their antics result in abuse they don't bother to hide their savage glee.

I lift my hands to the sky and close my eyes so the thread of communion and restoration this night builds can seep into me.

The bonfire is blazing high, and the few couples who still linger are enthralled by each other. I tilt my face again to the sky studded with stars. They gleam like tiny embers, and I watch in awe as some of them streak across the dark canvas. My body sways of its own accord to the distant thud of drums as I sip the flask of Burgundian wine. I wish he was here with me.

I've moved to the edge of the grove, cloaked in shadows, when strong arms circle my waist from behind. I tilt my head back further, so it's resting against his shoulder, and he sets his teeth against my earlobe.

My left arm reaches up and curves around his nape, anchoring him to me.

I can feel the imprint of each of his fingers, the barest touch below the weight of my breasts. I want them there, beneath the fabric. I've wanted it since our first kiss, and tonight I can set that desire free.

When I arch closer to him, he growls in response and fills his palm as I've been longing for him to do. The heat of it envelops me entirely, and liquid pools between my thighs. I shift restlessly against him, and he brushes his hand over the rigid peak of my breast.

"I think we are done here, mo chridhe fiadhaich. Tell me where I am carrying you." He rumbles into my ear.

"There's a byre just past the edge of the woods."

He hauls me into him, and I loop my arms around his neck. I feel the vibration of his laughter all the way to the tips of my toes when I rest my head against his chest.

"Your cheek is scorching the skin beneath my shirt."

"I was standing too close to the fire."

"If you say so, little witch."

He slows down as the trees thin. When I twist my neck, the byre is straight ahead. It's a rough three-sided structure open to the elements. It shouldn't look welcoming.

Dream fragments flit through my mind. I want to see the tattooed runes that cover his body. I want to map every scar and hollow of him. And I want the same courtesy.

He sets me on my feet and tugs me into the rough shelter. The ripe, sweet scent of hay surrounds us, and I sneeze when it tickles my nose. His laughter slides over my skin again as our bodies tumble together, until I'm braced above him, my skirts rucked up my thighs. I'm astride, my arms and legs akimbo, and I feel the hard ridge of him rise beneath me as he rolls his hips. One calloused palm slides up the bared length of my leg, skating over my calf, then my knee. He wraps it around the outer edge of my thigh and jerks me closer.

"We are alone, mo fiadhaich, with only the moon and the stars for company. And we will take advantage of it to the fullest. But first, I have a gift for you."

I glance toward the satchel he has slung around his waist. "You brought me more cheese?"

He laughs at my eagerness. "I brought us wine and cheese. Because I plan to exhaust you, leannan, and you will need sustenance. But no, that is not the gift."

He reaches into the satchel and pulls out a small bundle wrapped in oilskin. He reverently parts it to reveal a small harp.

My face falls. "It is beautiful, but I do not play."

He gives me a gentle smile. "The gift is not the harp. It is the song I will coax from its strings. A song for you and you alone. Come."

I take his outstretched hand and he lifts me atop one of the wooden carts. It's a comfortable berth filled with straw.

He crawls in beside me and leans against the hitch.

"Are songs always a part of your wooing?"

"Never. Until now. The music would not come to me. Until I spied you at your loom."

The first strum of his fingers sends a cascade of notes into the air that vibrate with such intensity I shiver. He cradles the harp and closes his eyes.

Those four notes were only a glimpse. The song is full of anguish and longing.

"*Mo chridhe fiadhaich. Wild heart of fire, wild soul of the wood that tames my beast. Mo chridhe fiadhaich, with eyes of green darkness and skin of snow and sunshine. Mo chridhe fiadhaich, I claim your wild heart. I claim your green darkness. I ask you to claim my beast.*"

When he opens his eyes and sets the harp aside, I clamber into his lap. I pepper kisses over his jaw and chin. "You wrote that for me?"

"Aye. I'm asking you to claim my beast. To let me make you mine tonight. To exchange the vows that have been lodged in my throat since the moment we met. To give me your body and your heart on this night when the world is made new, and it is only us."

I stroke a finger down the bridge of is nose before I cheerily peck its tip.

"And whatever creatures have found haven in this warm hay." I tease as I wrinkle my nose. "I thought you'd make your seduction more romantic."

He smiles. "I choose not to think of tiny claws and tiny teeth scrabbling and rustling around us."

"What do you choose to think of, mo stoirm, if not the wee beasties?"

He lies back and pulls me down, nuzzling my nose with his. "You. Only you. And all the waiting I have endured in anticipation of this moment. I don't want it to be over quickly, but my beast may have other ideas."

"You would let your beast overrule you?"

"Setting him free reveals my true nature. My true passion. The things I cannot live without and will fight to my last breath to protect."

"And I am one of those things?" The things he's vowed in the daylight feel more substantial on a night filled with stars and eldritch power.

"You know you are."

I moan when one of his hands slants possessively over my breast and he rolls the peaked tip between his thumb and forefinger. I've only felt the passing flash of his palm there before now, and I can't stifle my moan at the way this new caress feels.

"I want to feel the curve of your bare hips, and watch you arch above me. I need you to ride my beast, leannan. Every night I have feverish dreams of the sounds you'll make when I set my teeth against your throat."

"Yes."

My assent has barely left my mouth when his hands unclasp the belt around my outer tunic. He pushes it down to my elbows, and nimbly unravels the ties at the collar of my linen smock.

I try to push aside the collar of his tunic as well, but he's faster than me. He whips it over his head and bares the runes that decorate his body. I want to trace the intricate patterns with the pads of my fingers, and then with my tongue.

I reach forward and he presses a thumb to my lips. "Not yet, mo chridhe fiadhaich. I'm learning you first." I nip the tip of his thumb in retaliation and his gaze smolders, like a bonfire on the verge of shooting wild flames into the air. It raises goosebumps on my arms and makes me shiver.

He pushes the loosened smock from my shoulders, until it's snagged just over my bosom. He inhales, as if he's bracing himself, and tugs it to my waist. I'm not wearing a chemise, and my breasts rise and fall. The crystal pendant warms against my skin.

He's kneeling above me and he leans back, just watching. At least a handspan of minutes goes by without a word. I'm not what he expected. I swallow hard against the tears suddenly clogging my throat and lift my hands to cover myself.

He pushes them away, and finally looks up. "Och, leannan. You have no reason to weep." He flicks away the tears pooling in the corners of my eyes. "You are wondrous."

"You think me wondrous?" I am conscious of the map of scars on back.

"Aye. A creature crafted by the goddess to make me forget the world exists beyond this humble byre."

He kisses each knuckle and drops my hands.

I tremble as he leans closer, his breath feathering across my beaded nipples. It's warm against the chill of the stable. His hand curls around my talisman. "What is this?"

"It's from my mother. And her mother before her. I think it's for protection."

"It is for more than protection. Some of our seers wear crystals such as these. One this dark has been used to bind something inside it."

"Sometimes I see lights flickering in the heart of it. She gave it to me after she banished the eldritch king. Before she was too weak from the loss of blood."

"This is old magic. Even more reason for you to follow me home. You'll be able to converse with those who have more knowledge of these things."

"There are more interesting things to discuss than the purpose of the crystal I wear around my neck. What say you we discuss where I want to feel your mouth and hands?"

"I know what you want, mo chridhe." His lips slide down my throat and nip at the base.

I shift and moan restlessly beneath his touch. It feels like a jagged bolt of lightning is dancing through my veins.

"I knew you would whimper for my touch." His tongue swirls around the rim of my left areola and his wicked thumbnail flicks across its twin.

I arch into him, silently begging, as his mouth envelops me. He rumbles in response and digs his fingers into the flesh of my hip, urging me closer.

My hands flutter uselessly at my sides until I find the breadth of his shoulders in the dim light. I clasp him there as desperately as he's clasping my hip, scoring my nails against his flesh.

He chuckles against me. "The wee witch has claws."

"The better to mark you with."

"In retaliation or so we are equally claimed?" He sets his teeth against the upper curve of my breast, right against my birthmark. He nips the fold of skin, and there's a gentle suction.

This is his way of claiming me. When we leave this byre I'll bear the dark red imprint of him in the center of the mark I was born with.

"My turn." I stretch until my mouth rests on the hard curve of his shoulder. It's the beginning of the rune for courage that covers his arm. I gently nip the skin and return his suction. His body tenses and quivers beneath my assault.

When I'm satisfied he carries my mark, I lift my mouth to his.

He meets my plea with a smile, and the kiss is soft. My nails dig into the skin of his shoulders in protest because I need more pressure and savagery. His laughter rumbles against my lips and he takes heed.

There is nothing tender or sweet about this kiss. His teeth are sharp on my bottom lip and the corners of my mouth. They slide to my cheek and press a ferocious caress to the dimple of satisfaction there.

He tangles his fingers in my hair, pulling it loose to cascade between us. The slide of it over my chest as he bears me further into the hay, the whole weight of him crushing me, is exquisite. Our tongues wrangle provocatively, his stroking the roof of my mouth and mine flicking over the sharp edges of his teeth. I suck the end of his, a tug and invitation as earnest as the one I pressed into his skin. He rears back. "Och leannan, to feel your mouth around my cock like that." He punctuates his ragged confession with a thrust of his hips. I raise my hips in response, because I need to feel him stroke against the ache that is his fault.

"Not yet, wee witch." He hauls me closer and pulls my legs over his shoulders. "I want to taste ye first."

Those rasped words of longing are the only warning I receive. He envelops me, his tongue flicking against me in a steady rhythm. My limbs are tingling with something fizzy and languorous, as if I consumed an entire barrelful of mead. The nip of his teeth simultaneously stings and soothes, and the sweet, forbidden thrust of his tongue into the place that has known only my hand makes my toes point and arch behind his head.

All my flexing muscles seem to have a will of their own, awakened and desperate for any part of him they can reach. He sets the broad flat of his palm just below my navel, holding me in place. Everything is hazy under the cold moonlight that filters across our bodies, and his runes gleam like obsidian. Until they look like serpents writhing over the two of us as he devours me with wicked intent.

"Your taste is ambrosia."

The vibration of his voice against me as he feasts makes me tremble anew.

His tongue rasps against the tight marrow of my body, and he thrusts a finger inside me. His knuckle massages a place deep in my core, and I thrash against the invasion. I want more. I need more. But I don't know if I can withstand the pleasure of more.

He nips me harder this time, and something loosens the taut muscles of my stomach. My knees spasm and squeeze his ears as I thrash and convulse. I feel the gush of liquid and he growls in approval as he swallows it and licks me clean.

"Now." My voice is so hoarse I barely recognize it.

"Aye. Now."

And then he's above me, the runes like writhing serpents close enough to trace with my tongue.

"I know it may hurt."

He stills above me. "I will go slow, mo chridhe. So slow it will ease my passage and allow your body to welcome me to my home."

I snug my arms around his neck and press him down to me. When I playfully pucker my mouth for his, the kiss he gives me in answer is savage. I can almost feel the hooves of his beast pounding in his chest and the quartz is hot against my skin. Like an answering song of wildness and want.

He braces himself above me, and the crown of his cock breaches me body. He's barely inside me, and it's uncomfortable, but not painful. I squirm beneath him, and he groans. "I cannae go slow when ye move like that."

I do it again, because I can hear the cant of the islands in his voice, and it sounds like the tortured scrape of stone against stone. The threads of his control are unraveling, and I want them severed completely. With his surrender I will know he is fully mine.

I instinctively tense the muscles in my stomach and my core tightens around him. He slides in another inch, then two, then three. I imagine this is what it feels like to be poked by one of the swords hot from the forge. When it's been doused in water and the steam billows from it.

"Ye cannae make me laugh, fiadhaich. I will lose control."

"You knew what I was thinking?"

"Ofttimes it happens like that between mates, but that is not my power. Nae, ye spoke yer thoughts aloud."

I anchor my hands in his hair. "Lose control, mo stoirm. I can withstand it. Indeed, I am eager for it. And I am yours to claim."

With a groan, he drops his head to my shoulder. He bites the curve of it as he sinks all the way in.

There's a pinch of discomfort, and then it's gone. All I feel is him. I'm surrounded by his scent, and I wonder if my stepfather will smell it on me tomorrow and ask why our home reeks of the sea stench. I wonder if I'll be able to blame it on the cod.

"Ye laugh again. Albeit in silence. What do ye find so amusing about my lovemaking, song of my heart?"

My laughter is suddenly on the brink of tears. "Song of my heart?"

He eases out and pistons back into me. So forcefully the ankles I didn't even realize I crossed behind his back fly apart. "Aye, song of my heart. Tell me why you were laughing."

I giggle again. "I simply wonder if I will smell like you on the morrow."

He grins triumphantly. "Thoroughly bedded with the musk and sweat of love between us?"

"Something akin to that. That first day, my stepfather claimed he could smell the noxious odor of the sea."

He stills inside me, and an incredulous expression crosses his face. "He called me noxious?"

"Not you specifically. Just the aroma. I blamed it on the cod peddler."

This time the rumble of his laughter joins mine. "Ye cannae ever tell Callum of your fib. He will ne'er let me forget it."

I shuffle upward and nuzzle his ear. "You don't smell like cod, my love. You smell like the sting of salt when the wind is whipping the waves into a frenzy and the sky is shifting to the dark blue of a storm."

He grunts. "Well, that is a more flattering comparison than cod."

"I'll think of more if you finish what you've begun, prince."

He lifts me, so his hand is braced against the small of my back. His eyes darken when he feels the ridged web of scars. "You will tell me of these later so I may seek retribution."

He folds my knees under with his other hand, and I am like wet clay for him to mold and shape. When I am spread wide enough for his liking, he raises himself to his knees and thrusts into my arched body.

His eyes are the deep dark of a moonless night, his features taut as he rears back. His gaze scours and abrades me as he plunges forward. The pulse and scrape of his conquest is like the serrated edge of a blade hovering between blinding pleasure and pain exquisitely wrought.

He pinches my breast and circles my wrists. I am covered by his skin and bound by his merciless touch. In this moment as he roars and spills his seed inside me, I am more wholly his than I have ever been.

Chapter Eleven

Eachann

My cock pulses inside her as if it's a separate appendage with a life of its own. It wants to live there, nestled within her warmth and wonder forever, just as my beast and I long to do. Now that she has fully given herself to me, there will never be any other.

She is a dewy, tousled goddess in my arms. The scrape of my beard against her body left its mark. The wings above her breast carry the imprint of my teeth. My seed still empties into the welcoming clasp of her womb.

"I will allow you a fortnight, mo chridhe fiadhaich."

"A fortnight for what?" She drowsily asks.

"A fortnight to prepare for your departure. It is too dangerous for you here. The scars on your back belie the truth of your situation. Now that you are fully mine, I will let none tear us asunder or raise a hand against you."

"We've exchanged no vows."

"We exchange them now. When we have shared the abundance of our bodies as we will share the abundance and triumph of our lives."

"We bind ourselves in the old way, not the new."

"Aye. Those vows mean nothing to me or my kin. I, Eachann Lir, Prince of the Each Uisge of the North Sea and Lord of the Far Realms, pledge to protect and honor my mate. To give her my shield and cloak, my unwavering loyalty and the wild heart of my beast."

"What are my vows to be?"

"You must pledge to accept my protection and honor me in turn, to shelter behind my shield and don my cloak, and to tame my beast."

She places her hand over my heart, over the rune for eternity. "I vow to accept your protection. I vow to find shelter in the strength of your shield and the warmth of your cloak. I vow to tame your beast." She slides her hand up my chest and cups my jaw. "And I vow to be your home."

The awe of her overwhelms me and I clasp her so tightly it's a wonder I do not break her. "I vow you are the only home I've ever truly wanted."

I want us to lie here beneath the quiet, star-laden night and exchange our secrets. I want us to emerge from this byre with our clasped hands swinging between us, never to be parted again.

But we are still bound by a chain of stolen moments.

We dress slowly. Because I sneak kisses, and her hands flit over the canvas of my runes. I tangle my fingers in hers as I lead her to the edge of the forest.

She wraps her arms around my waist and her bowed head comes to rest against the heart that beats only for her.

"I do not want to go. Every parting is harder."

"Aye. Each one is an arrow dipped in sweet poison, binding me more closely to you and filling my blood with a longing that slowly overtakes it. A fortnight, mo chridhe."

"I do not know…"

I place my finger against her lips and harden my expression. "A fortnight. I cannot bear the thought of you there when there is the possibility of more of this." I lightly graze her back.

Not even the flat of Callum's sword against my shin can spoil my mood. I finally claimed my mate in every way that counts. I know her body. Every freckle. The winged birthmark above her heart and the divots of her elbows. I heard the tinkle of her laughter as I tickled her stomach with a day's worth of beard.

We pledged our troth to each other in the ancient words of my kind. Though we did so without a sigil ceremony, it feels no less real or necessary. I am changed. Forever tethered to her.

"You're hopeless today." Callum tosses his sword away in disgust.

"He's in love. He's not only hopeless, he's useless." Carrig chimes in.

"Aye. I'm in love with my mate, whose body is fairer than that of Fionnuala and whose heart is truer than any of you lot."

"Ye've had her then? Did ye take precautions, ye fool?"

"She'll wear my sigil. There is no need for precaution."

Carrig's low whistle is accompanied by Callum's hiss. "Ye know what it will mean if ye've anticipated yer oath. Ye endanger all of us."

"The gods will not send the sea to swallow our kingdom because I have taken my mate. Those are no more than tales we are told to keep us obedient."

"Ye cannae know that. 'Tis one of the oldest taboos we have. Ye cannae plant yer seed in yer mate until they bear yer sigil. 'Tis the only way to harness our beasts."

"My beast has been naught but her servant since the day we met."

"The taboo is part of our culture for a reason." Carrig protests.

His creased forehead belies his concern. He tends to act like a fussy nursemaid before he launches into a lecture. He is the scholar among us. Callum and I still don't know why he chose iron over words. We both suspect it has more to do with our fiery sister than anything else.

"You are the one that has pored over our history and legends. Why is paying heed to the taboo so important?"

"The stories tell us that when we ignore it and obey our whims instead, the beast becomes the dominant part of our nature. Once we are mated, we must bind his power. If we do not, his form becomes the only one we have. That is why we have the sigil ceremony."

"My beast and I are in harmony."

"You tempt the gods to prove you wrong. We are the children of Lir, and we constantly seek harmony with our beasts and their base urges. The ceremony is a way to ensure those base urges do not wreak havoc or sow chaos."

Callum chuckles. "Enough, brehon."

We call our friend this when we think he's being too pompous. Because he sounds like one of the dour judges.

"Aye, enough brehon. You worry too much."

"And the two of you don't worry enough," he sharply replies.

"I worry plenty. I worry about where to find the best mead and the most willing partner." Callum grins darkly.

Carrig rolls his eyes. "We all know you have more substance than that. No matter what you profess."

I throw my arm around Carrig's shoulder. "Yea, now that I have a mate to protect, I worry about far more."

My brother snorts. "It's about time you worried about more than filling your gullet and emptying your seed."

"My gullet, maybe. But you're the one who never keeps a partner in your bed for more than one night."

"Becoming emotionally attached makes a warrior weak and vulnerable to attack."

Callum takes his role as the head of our armies and my personal guard far too seriously. I know he thinks me shallow and idiotic sometimes, but it is only that I wish to savor the marrow of life.

"You must tell father. Without delay. If you don't do it soon, I'll do it for you. Your silence endangers the kingdom and I have been entrusted with its protection."

My brother has had a sword in his hand since we were nine summers. He was drawn to iron and I was drawn to music. I always wanted to sit at the feet of the bards and he always wanted to run around the training field.

Father has me so involved in the running of the kingdom I no longer have time for music. At least not for composition.

I don't avoid conflict – but neither do I seek it out. I place more value in deflating a situation than I do in enflaming it. We are a society of warriors and there is always a dispute to resolve.

Chapter Twelve

Galanta

There is little I will miss of this village.

But I will miss the green embrace of the forest and the whisper of the leaves. I will miss the feel of the rough bark beneath my hands as I gather strength and courage.

My menses were due last week. And they have not come. This morning, the crystal hummed against my skin – as if it sensed the change at work in my body. I know the proof of our love grows in my womb. Though I will miss the trees, I will go with him to his kingdom of sand and windswept rock. I will not jeopardize the fate of our child.

I am stepping into the narrow alley that opens to the forest path when someone grabs my elbow.

"Girl, your recklessness will mean your death. Do you want to burn at the stake?" The older woman hisses at me in disbelief.

Mairead was my mother's childhood friend. She's done what she can since my mother's death. She untied me from the whipping post once when the priest was otherwise occupied, and she's brought me extra gruel and salve when my infractions have been deemed deserving of confinement in the hole beneath the chapel.

When she places her hand on my arm, I meet her troubled gaze. Her eyes are keen on mine and her grip is tight as she pulls me into the shadows between the forge and the granary. "Lass, I'm warning you because of the affection I bore your mother. The tavern wench hovers on the cusp of death, and I pray for your sake you had naught to do with it. You have been reckless – there are those who spotted you paying a visit to her cottage after she fell ill."

"I'm careful." I am always careful. Because I know one misstep could mean my doom.

"Not careful enough. Some of us who gather mussels in the evening have seen you leaving the grove trailed by one of our enemy. And none will lift a finger to save you if your womb swells with that demon seed. Their kind are banished from the eye of God for a reason and you're foolish for falling under their spell. If any of the men catch you, they'll slaughter him and let the ravens pick both your bones clean."

"They may be dangerous, but so are we. These creatures you think so abhorrent are less evil than some of those who live in this village."

"They are an abomination in the eyes of God. You should sever whatever this is before it leads to your doom."

Her expression is earnest, not judgmental. She means no harm. She seems to truly believe Father Mulcahy's vitriol. She makes her warning with the best of intentions and is urging caution because she doesn't wish to see me burned for witchcraft.

"I thank you for your concern, Mairead. I will take heed of it."

My placation has the desired effect. She relaxes her grip on my arm and steps away. "It would behoove ye to do so."

She makes her way to the end of the narrow street and glances in each direction before stepping forward. Was she checking for witnesses? Has it come to that? Am I truly so reviled that merely being seen in my presence condemns others?

I shake my head to clear it and make for the opposite end of the alley that leads to the edge of the forest.

Is the quickening of my womb so obvious, or was she only warning me of the consequences of such an outcome?

He grabs my hands as soon as I'm close enough to touch. He's bending his head and I know I'll lose my ability to focus, so I lay the flat of my palm on his jaw. "I have something to tell you."

"Can it not wait, mo chridhe faidhaich? I ache for your touch."

"And your aching is why we need to talk," I snap.

"My aching? Do you have other ways to assuage it?"

"No. Your aching had consequences."

His face floods with fear and then his eyes glint with determination. "Someone saw us. You will come with me now."

"No one saw us," I reassure him. "But I am carrying our child."

His boisterous laughter fills the glade. He lifts me into his arms and twirls me about. His joy is infectious, and my laughter joins his.

He sets me down with a somber expression. "My father needs to break my betrothal. I'll claim none but you."

I close my eyes. I have no one to tell that will welcome the tidings. Their reaction will be the opposite of joy, and I'll be labeled a whore as well as a witch. "I think we should keep it between ourselves. Unless you can trust the counsel of your brother."

He tips my chin up and searches my gaze. "This is a blessing from the gods and goddesses, leannan. We should rejoice in it and each other."

"My heart is filled with terror, but I am still rejoicing. I live in fear of what will happen if our consort is discovered. I have seen enough loss to fear childbirth itself. I fear becoming a mother when I no longer have a mother to learn from."

"I am here, and from this moment on I have no other purpose than to care for you and our babe. You will bear nothing alone. Once I convince my father that the selkie wedding is now out of the question, my family will be forced to accept you. You will have a home and a family when we welcome our babe into the world."

"We are not truly wed. In the eyes of this village, I have anticipated my vows and am unclean."

"That is not the way of each uisge. We have only anticipated the sigil ceremony and that is easily rectified."

"I do not want us to begin our parenthood estranged from those you love."

"My mother will persuade my father that this is everything I want and the only path for me. I will speak to her soon." He lifts me into his arms. "But not now. Now I wish only to show my mate how desperately I have craved her touch. I have a blanket strapped beneath my swords, beloved."

Chapter Thirteen

Eachann

I will not allow Callum and Carrig's dire warnings to ring in my head. Children are a blessing the gods bestow on us and our son will be cherished despite the timing of his conception. Our love will ensure he isn't tainted with berserker wildness or harnessed to his beastly form and no other.

My mate's laughter fills the glade and every crevice of my heart. I reluctantly set her down and release the scabbards from my back. The blanket roll falls to the ground and I kneel to unfold it beneath the shelter of the sacred oak.

Once I relocate the bits of bramble and rock that will make our union uncomfortable, I recline and extend my hand. "Join me here."

She falls to her knees beside me, and I clamp her body against mine. She gasps when my tented arousal scrapes against her. That gasp is the entrance I sought, and my kiss echoes the desperation that has been my boon companion since I last cradled her to me.

My tongue strokes hers with fierce intent, every tangle and tug a reminder of the way we devastate and remake each other. Her hands fumble with the belt around my waist that secures the flask of wine and hunk of cheese she has come to expect. I remove her hands.

"Let me show you how my body would welcome you, leannan."

"Yea, show me prince."

I swiftly unclasp the belt and toss it aside. I lift the hem of my shirt and it joins the discarded pile.

"There was only moonlight and I could not appreciate these as I wished the first time you bared them to me." Her mouth drops to my runes.

She nibbles at them. Like they are a delicate feast she wants to savor.

"I am not one of your wheels of cheese, woman."

"Nay, you taste much better," she murmurs as her tongue rasps against the flat coin of my nipple. She sets her teeth there, the nip sharp and sweet. Her hand falls between my spread legs and molds the fabric there. She kneads the length of my cock with a wicked glint in her eye.

"You will unman me."

"That is my intention."

She retreats just enough to sink further down, her hands anchored to the jut of my hips. Her hot breath coasts over my navel as she sets the flat of her tongue against the whorl of dark blond that disappears into my trews.

She rears to her knees and yanks the kirtle over her head. Her hair falls when she wrests the clothing out of the way. It's a tumbling waterfall of fire and I want to see it caress the rosy pink of tips of her breasts.

She fumbles with the strings of her bliaut. When they become knotted, she huffs in frustration.

"Let me." I push her hands aside and lower my head.

The length of knotted string snaps easily at the gnash of my teeth. I push the gown just beneath the swan's curve of her neck and shoulders. She wriggles and it slips further, hovering precariously on the cusp of revelation. One more shiver of her body and that flaming hair will caress the bare, rosy peaks of her breasts.

I lay the flat of my hand against her sternum and let the aching tension spiral between us. Her heart thumps beneath my touch like that of a frightened fawn. She braces her hands behind her and bows her back. The supple bend makes the fabric fall to her waist. I wrap the tendrils of scarlet around my wrist and slip my other hand beneath her skirts. She moans when I brush the bud of her arousal. She's scarlet there too.

I press against her inner thighs and her knees fall open on either side of me. She's wet and wide open. My cock is harder than the blade of my sword and I want to sheathe it in my mate. She was made for me, and I want to savor her surrender.

She is slick beneath my touch and her desire coats my fingers when I sink them into her channel. She jerks in my hold and moans as I thrust in and out, flicking my thumb against her on every pass.

"Now, prince."

"Now what, witch?"

The sharp points of her nails dig into my shoulders. "You cannot show me the stars and think I'll be content with anything less. Make me feel like I'm yours."

I drop my forehead to hers. "Mine." I kiss the apples of her cheeks, the golden smatter of each freckle, the corners of her eyelids. Her solitary dimple. The bow of her mouth stained with the dark purple juice of the berries she's so fond of.

She closes her eyes and slides her hands to my elbows. "That's more like it."

"Are you going to return the favor?"

Her eyes flicker open. "Yes."

I flip us over, so I'm the one on the bottom. Her knees are snug against my hips, and she hovers just above me. "I want to watch." I lift her skirts and fist my hands in them – so there's nothing obscuring my view.

"I want that too," she murmurs. She gives me a coquettish glance from beneath her lids and sets her nimble fingers to the wooden buttons. My cock strains against the opening, and springs eagerly toward her as soon as the space and opportunity present themselves.

She curls her hand around me, her eyes full of heat and wonder. I groan when her finger swipes the leaking tip and she sucks it between her berry-stained lips with a subtle pop. She leans on her haunches and shakes her hair out of the way. It cascades down her back, so she's fully bared to me. One greedy hand strokes down my chest. "Mine." She growls like a kitten at play.

"Yours." I agree. "If you follow the arrow, you'll find your reward."

She traces the path of hair that bisects my chest. All the way to the part of me that's most desperate for her. She finally sinks all the way against me. When I grasp her hips she shakes her head and begins easing away. "You said you wanted me to show you that you're mine. That means you have to let me take control. I'm the one staking my claim, not you. No controlling our pace or using your strength to move me about like a straw doll. Let me enjoy my ride, prince."

She's a merciless, fiendish bean sidhe.

She braces her hands behind her, so they're splayed over my thighs, and lowers her body one agonizing inch at a time. When I'm fully seated, she begins to move. She grinds herself against the base of my cock with every slide. Her eyes are closed in ecstasy and when she sets her own hands to her breasts and shudders over me like a ship tossed about by a storm, I know she's close to release.

"Yours." I growl as I punch my hips up. She clenches all the way around my length and looks down at me with eyes that are the jade of the trees around us. Glittering and dark and possessive.

"Yea, mine." In an echo of my caress, she presses soft lips to the bridge of my nose and the edge of one eyebrow. She collapses onto my chest as I spill inside her.

"I could sleep just as we are."

I smile at her drowsy confession. "As could I. Soon we'll have that luxury. And the comfort of a real mattress. Not scratchy straw or the hard ground."

"'Tis something I eagerly anticipate."

"You must leave before your condition is recognized."

She rolls away from me and groans. "I'm grateful I am the one who prepares the morning meal. And that I do it well before they rise. The sickness is the worst then – before I've had a morsel of bread to settle my stomach."

"You needn't hide once you accompany me."

"Good. I grow weary of hiding." She turns to face me, her hands clasped beneath her cheek. "I hide who I am, who and what I want. I hide what I wish for and what I would destroy if I could do so without fear of retaliation."

"What would my bloodthirsty mate like to destroy?"

"I would burn the chapel to the ground. Mayhap with Father Mulcahy inside it. I think the goddess would forgive me."

"She most certainly would. She is the goddess of war after all."

"Am I terrible for wanting his demise?"

"No. He has shown you nothing but cruelty. I do not believe in turning the other cheek."

"Would you gallop to my rescue if things went awry?"

I smooth the curls away from her forehead. "You know I would. Once you have my sigil carved into the skin of your wrist, all you'll have to do to summon me is place your fingers over it and call the name of my each uisge. It is how I'll protect you when we're apart."

"Is it used often?"

"Yes, especially in time of war. Are you afraid you'll require my assistance soon, leannan?"

Her brow creases in worry. "One of my mother's bosom friends sought me out today."

"Because she needed your assistance?"

"No. She sought me out to warn me. The woman I treated hangs onto her life by a mere thread. And someone spotted you following me from the glade."

"You need to have your belongings ready at a moment's notice." When the unrest simmering below the surface boils over, she'll have nowhere to run. "Can you row?"

"I can manage if I need to. Why?"

"I'll hide a boat in one of the coves on the far side of the island. You may need it sooner than you realize."

"I am frightened of what is to come. What if my dreams of salt and fire are on the verge of becoming true? What if the love we feel was doomed from the moment we met?"

"If our love is doomed, it is doomed. I wouldn't trade the handful of moments I've had with you for a lifetime of safety."

"Nor would I." She quietly assures me as she lays her hand over my heart.

Chapter Fourteen

Galanta

My brothers' leman died four nights ago. Their eyes have been red-rimmed, and their inconsolability almost moves me to sympathy. Her death has been attributed to a fever she caught from one of the traders.

Her name has yet to be linked to my own, and the whispered rumors being exchanged about my visit to her cottage haven't surfaced.

Since her death and burial in the churchyard, the ravens have grown more persistent. When I walk past their roost, they flap their wings thrice before launching into the air above my head. They swoop and circle above me, a living crown of feathers. I should be grateful for the protection my mate assured me they were offering, but the way they follow me feels portentous.

I cannot help but wonder if the way they stalk my steps is a warning of things to come. If their hoarse admonition is a reminder to beware. I decide to staunchly ignore the squawking of the birds. Whatever message they are here to deliver will not reach my ears.

My mother told me little of what service to Morrigan entailed and I don't know what's expected of me other than honoring the festivals and placing my offerings of honey and oats in the glade when the moon waxes full. The crystal around my neck burnt my skin whenever I laid my hand on the tattered pages of the family grimoire. It wanted me to unlock whatever mysteries it held. I knew those mysteries would consume me, and unlock the power my mother bade me to keep hidden. I hid it beneath the trees and buried it beneath layers of dirt and leaves after she died. I haven't sought it out since that day. My stepfather is unfamiliar with the language of the runes but would have recognized it is far more than a collection of folk wisdom.

I have denied every part of my heritage but the legacy of healing since I buried that book.

There have been rumblings of discontent in the village all week, and as more and more children are taken by the sickness that covers our village like a cloud of doom, the rumbles grow more strident. I cannot afford to be seen conversing with ravens or cavorting with an enemy of my kind.

I know the risks and I cannot stay away.

Every evening I sneak into the cloak of the forest and let the grove hold my secret. Every evening I creep around the edges of buildings and skulk in the shadows between the houses to escape notice. My stepfather attributes my frequent absences to the insidious spread of disease, and I do not correct him. I ensure the basket always dangling from my grasp is never empty when I return from my trysts.

I always find mo stoirm waiting for me in the grove. His hands braced on his hips, his gaze intent on the blurred line where the sky meets the sea. I know being this far from the embrace of saltwater makes him weaker. I can sense his unease and know what his sacrifice is worth.

This evening his brow is creased with worry. I've given him no cause to fret and have kept my mounting fears close to my breast - so he isn't compelled to confront their source. For the first time in my life, I felt the scatter of pebbles glance off my shoulder this morning as I made my way to the bedside of one of my patients. When I whirled around to seek out the culprit, I heard a whispered witch and the skitter of running feet. The voice was that of a child and I know children absorb what they hear. The attack was only a mimicry of the dark mutterings of the adults in their household. If they have begun to call me cursed and witch behind closed doors, I shouldn't risk meeting him here. I should tread with caution instead of recklessness.

I cannot stay away. Especially now I know our union at Bealtaine bore fruit and our babe grows in my womb.

"Mo chridhe fiadhaich. Every evening you arrive later than the one before. I feared something had befallen you."

He pulls me into his embrace, and I rest my cheek against the steady thud of his heart.

"Nothing would keep me away. I am late because I must take every precaution to ensure we are not found out."

"Is anyone suspicious?"

"No, I think I have allayed any suspicions they harbored. That will be impossible once my womb quickens enough to show."

"When will you leave with me?"

I lift my hand to his cheek. "Soon. I will have to leave before the babe is born. If its parentage is revealed, the priest will deem it a changeling and demand I rid myself of it. Either before our child is born or by exposing it to the elements after the birth."

"We cannot hide much longer. The selkie princess visits our court in two moons and we begin negotiations. I will have to tell my father that I have given my heart to another. That I'll accept no one else."

"We have time to convince him."

He sighs against the crown of my head, ruffling the tendrils of hair escaping my braid and curling over my ears. "I grow weary of this deception. I want the world to know that you are mine and I am yours. That those who do not deserve your care and time, who do not appreciate it, claim more of you than I can, drives me mad with jealousy."

"You have no reason to be jealous – even when I am with them, my heart goes wherever you go."

"I have every reason to be jealous, witch. I am jealous of the sun that touches your shoulders when I cannot. I am jealous of the rain that feathers kisses across your lips when

I cannot. I am jealous of the moonlight that bathes your body as my mouth wishes to do."

"We have time." I reassure him.

"I've found the site for our fortress."

"We won't live at the keep with your family?"

"My father may banish us from his sight. And I've been surrounded by my huge brood of an extended family my whole life. I want a place just for us."

"Why would your father banish us?"

"You carry my seed but you do not carry my sigil. We have acted in defiance of ceremonial order. My father will view my disregard of tradition as an inexcusable insult."

My pulse flutters in alarm. "What will he do?"

"He'll roar and stomp about and my mother will have to soothe his beast. But he only wants Callum, Sabhinion and I to find happiness with our true mates. And I have. He won't be angry for long."

"But while he is we should keep our distance?"

"Aye."

"And you truly believe he'll come to accept your decision?"

"If he doesn't want me to abdicate my claim to the throne, he will. I'm not giving you up."

"Can't your brother take your place if you're forced to renege your claim?"

"Callum has never wanted to rule. He's far more comfortable with a sword in his grip than a scepter. He wants to be on the ground leading the charge, not sitting on a hill watching from the distance. He is a true warlord, not merely a general."

"So one of you was groomed to rule and the other was trained to kill."

"Our father chose our paths for us – we do not resent them but neither one of us can help wondering if there is more. Especially Callum. He is strategic when I am rash, wise when I am impulsive. He would have made a better ruler even though he wants nothing of the sort."

"Is there a law of primogeniture? Can your father's decision be set aside?"

"I am the eldest, so yes, the throne is mine by default. But Callum has no patience for the machinations of court. He is too blunt."

"Then we will abide by your father's decision and depend on his blessing."

"What of your family? Have you told them our news?"

"No. And I shan't. They are completely unaware of our liaison and none of them are of my blood. My father died when I was an infant and my mother never spoke of him. My stepfather raised me and my stepbrothers accompanied him to our hearth when he wed my mother."

Chapter Fifteen

Eachann

When Callum and I return to the keep, I set off to find our mother. When I do, she is in the far tower, absorbed in tapestry work with a gaggle of her handmaidens. She takes in my expression and immediately dismisses her companions.

"What is it, my son?"

"I have fallen in love."

She sets aside her needlework. "And your love is not the bride your father has chosen for you. She could not be. You've yet to make her acquaintance, at least the woman she is now. You only knew her as a girl."

"No. I am in love with a mortal. A healer from the largest village." I take a deep breath because I need to tell her everything my mate is. "And a witch."

Her forehead wrinkles in dismay. "A healer? We can always use one with that knowledge to serve our people. But a witch? We have a long history of treachery and mistrust where witches are concerned. Even in the dark northern forests of my homeland that are their domain, they are not to be trusted."

"She is persecuted for her skills, not revered or feared."

My mother frowns. "She is feared. Otherwise they would not persecute her. What manner of witch is she?"

"She is a green witch. A daughter of forest and field."

"So she knows naught of the sea. You know those who love the forest are anathema to our kind. More so than mere mortals. She has eldritch in her blood, and it fears the brine in ours."

"We feel anything but fear for one another."

She sets her hand on my wrist, her gaze troubled. "You are sure of this?"

"More certain than I have ever been. Of anything."

"And you sought me out because you need me to intervene on your behalf," she concludes with a wry smile.

"Father will be more amenable to my pleas if you're the one to tell him."

She snorts delicately. "He's worked for years to secure the alliance with the selkies. Nothing will make him amenable. But I may be able to appease him if I remind him of our own love story."

She was taken as a hostage by my father when her family attacked our keep. She is of northern heritage and gave me her fair complexion and golden yellow hair. Her family were marauders determined to steal our riches. My father took one look at her standing in the prow of her brother's ship and offered a bargain. All the gold they could carry in their biggest ship in exchange for their sister.

Her brothers enthusiastically agreed. She would have been a queen in her own right and was not eager to bind her fate to a mysterious kingdom at the edge of the world. My father spent an entire year wooing her before she finally surrendered. The bards still regale us with the ode composed in their honor.

"Thank you, mother."

She cups my cheek in her palm. "You are welcome, my golden boy. I will convince your father to let you choose your own path."

I cover my relief with a kiss to the crown of her head. "I knew you would understand."

I am bent over an old ballad I found in the library when my father approaches me. It's in the Old Elvish tongue, so the translation is taking me longer than I thought it would. I want to arrange it for the harp and play it for her.

Though I sang for her, I haven't told her about my music. Because I never seem to have time for it anymore, and the songs have been quiet for years. Until now. Until her.

"You hear the music again."

"Aye. It feels like it never left."

"Is she the reason?"

I nod. "The songs came back the first time I heard her voice. She's what they were waiting for."

My father sighs. "If you are making music again, the gods have spoken. You should have told me earlier, lad.

'Twill be difficult to break off bride price negotiations with the selkie queen."

"You are not angry."

"No, son. I'm saddened by your lack of trust, but I am not angry." His gaze is somber, and he looks careworn. The hint of gray at his temples seems more visible this night, his shoulders not as broad as they once were. Although we each uisge live for millennia, the burdens he's carried for so long are finally revealed in his countenance.

"I was certain you'd be furious."

"Your mother forbade it. When she first told me I wanted to find you and wring your neck. You could not have chosen a stonier path to happiness than this one. I chose my own stony path, so I know of what I speak."

"We have already professed our love for one another. I need not spend a year wooing her to my side."

"Ah, son. Your mother was worth the frustration of all that wooing. And we had time to build things between us before we made you and your twin. From what your mother has told me, you do not have that luxury."

"We have exchanged vows, but not sigils."

"I should be angry that you have openly defied millennia of tradition. My first reaction was one of fury. I would have banished you from my sight if I had come to you then. You were wise to let your mother intervene on your behalf."

"We all see the way you still look at her. I want that with my mate. I could not bind myself to the selkie princess when my green witch holds my heart in her hands."

"It would not have been fair to either one of you. But the selkie queen has long coveted a foothold in our kingdom, and your marriage was how she chose to pursue it. She will demand that foothold, regardless of the broken troth."

"What will happen if we cannot meet her demands?"

He laughs harshly. "You know what will happen, Eachann. War. A war we can ill afford. Our kingdom is riven in two by the unrest your uncle has been sowing. There are those who grumble I do not know how to navigate this new world, and my rule is causing more harm than good."

"Everything you've done has been for the good of all those who live in these waters."

"They do not see it that way. They see the riches the selkies flaunt because of trade. They care more for furs and gold than they do for independence. They do not see the consequences of relying on the charity and beneficence of others. What will we trade for their wares when we have taught them to harvest pearls and the other treasures of the sea?"

"What have you foreseen?"

"No seer has come to me with a vision of devastation if that is what you are asking. But I saw how the horde of Rome descended on the tribes across the water. How it crested over them like a great wave, until everything they stood for was either submerged or absorbed. Their identities lost, their gods forsaken and their traditions forgotten."

"Perhaps our court does not understand what is at stake."

"Or they choose to ignore it. Every debate I have with your uncle becomes more heated. I fear things will soon be wrested from my control."

"You should request more guards instead of worrying over your headstrong son."

"You are my heir. When this conflict Cairneach is determined to incite reaches its tipping point, your future will be affected. Every parent worries over whether their children are equipped to inherit the world they leave behind."

"You suspect your brother will take the kingdom from you at the cost of your life."

"Half of your brother's army has already pledged its loyalty to him. And Riordan informed me he overheard the courtiers discussing the benefits of aligning themselves with him."

"Though political wrangling is not my strength, even I see the tempest barreling toward us."

"It will be a tempest. You need to bring your mate here as soon as you are able so we can protect her. If she carries your seed, she becomes a target for your uncle's greed."

"She carries my seed. I was afraid to tell you that too. Because it is a violation of our sacred rituals."

"I'll not lie about my trepidation. The rituals have been in place for as long as our kind has inhabited these islands. They were forged as both protection and to strengthen our ties to the gods. Impregnating your mate before you are both protected by the sanctity of the sigil ceremony was reckless."

"We exchanged vows, just not sigils."

"The sigils are what ensure the bond is unbreakable." He pulls me into a one-armed hug. "I'm happy for ye, lad, just be wary. Have you told your mother?"

"I wanted to tell you first."

"She wants nothing more than to welcome her grandchildren into the world. Even if your love means maintaining order will grow more difficult, I rejoice in your happiness because 'twill make your mother happy as well."

Chapter Sixteen

Galanta

The cottage is dank, and smells of stale sweat. Mairead, my mother's childhood friend and the thatcher's wife, lies on the straw mattress in the corner. She is sleeping for now, her body curled protectively around her youngest daughter. They are snuggled under a bundle of furs.

I turn to Lianth. She is the oldest and the one that sent the summons. "How long?"

"Too long. The fever has raged nigh on four days. The priest's benediction has had no effect, and he bade us ready them for burial."

I gently pat her arm. "They are still with us and battling the infection."

"This is like no other. The blisters cover their skin, and their tongues are so swollen they can barely swallow more than a trickle of water."

Lianth speaks truth. The latest sickness overwhelming the village is a gift from the merchants who were here two weeks ago. It's already claimed nine of us, including two young, strong men who seemed invincible.

This plague is almost a certain death, and when the pustules burst on their skin, the end is near. Mairead and her youngest are hanging on, but we are at a crossroads. I extract the feverfew from my satchel. "Do you have any boiled water?"

She nods. "Yes. I've kept the pot over the hearth full. I will pour some into Mam's mug so you can steep the herbs."

She's assisted me during several of her mother's deliveries, so she knows exactly what's required. "We'll start with the tea. But we need to cool them down."

"How?" She wrings her hands in desperation.

"Cold seawater will do the trick, but we must be extremely gentle when we lay the cloths on their brows."

"I'll send Seamus."

Seamus is normally a mischievous, inquisitive child, but his expression is grave. "Aye, I'll fetch it." He dips his head in a salute of respect and runs full tilt out the door.

I place a hand on Lianth's forearm. "I will do all I can."

"I wanted to summon you before now, but my father wouldn't allow it. But he's in the tavern drowning his sorrows and I know you are the only hope we have."

"Your father wouldn't allow it?" I thought he was tolerant of my efforts if not supportive. I have safely delivered every one of his children. Either at the side of my mother or by myself once she was gone.

"The priest insists that the prayer is the only cure we should seek, and if it doesn't work, whatever happens is God's will. He's been proclaiming that the hands of a woman are not meant to interfere in what they do not understand. That altering the course of life is nothing more than an evil conjuring."

I knew the priest disapproved of my vocation and was intent on discrediting me. But I was unaware how persuasive his vitriol has been to his parishioners. "Then I must do all I can to wrest them from the reaper's grasp."

I kneel beside the bed and lift Mairead's head so I can tip the mug toward her parched lips. I have to massage the unbroken skin of her throat to ease the liquid down. She splutters, and the drops wet the front of my dress. I tip the cup again. And again. And again. Until it's empty.

When I move to the other side to do the same for Lianth's three-year-old sister, my efforts are futile. The child's body is limp in my arms, and her skin is cold marble to the touch. "She is gone."

Lianth breaks into a sob before biting her lip. "My foolish father. This is his fault."

"Nay. The sickness may have taken her despite my care. Her body was weak and the fever was strong."

"He and the priest will heap the blame on your shoulders."

"This was not my doing."

Lianth wrings her hands. "I know that. But I acted against his wishes and when he set out this mid-morning, they were both still alive."

"You must wrap her in a shroud and burn her clothing. I will do everything in my power to see your mother defeat this."

She lays a palm against her mother's brow and sweeps her hair from her forehead. "She is what holds us together."

"I know. Do as I've asked. I'll deliver the news to your father."

I don't move from Mairead's bedside. My eyes are heavy, my hands tremble, and my mind is racing. All night I keep my vigil. I plead with the Goddess to show mercy. There is so little kindness left in this harsh village. And Mairead has always been my champion. I recall the way she warned me weeks ago and I know she has kept my secret. I would have been immediately hauled in front of the priest. She is one of the few remaining villagers who pays occasional homage to the old ways, and she's instilled those beliefs in her children.

I wake to someone shaking my shoulder and tugging at my skirts. I blink my eyes open and brush away the grit that feels like it's coated on my lashes. "What has happened?"

"Father's finally on his way home and he's roaring mad. Someone told him about Caitie's death and your presence. You need to leave."

"But what about your mother?" I ask as I lurch to my feet.

"She is on the mend thanks to you. I will gladly face his wrath for my decision to bring you here. But I don't want you harmed."

"Let me gather my things," I mumble as I slip on my pattens.

"I've already done that for you." She slides the strap of my satchel over my shoulder. "You should be on your way while it's clear."

When I return to the cottage, I'm unsettled by all that's transpired. I'm ladling porridge into bowls for my stepfather and stepbrothers when there's an infernal knocking on the door. I swing it open to the smirking priest. He's flanked by four of the village elders. Bearded, grizzled men who regularly come to my door for joint salve. At least they look sheepish.

The priest dangles a ball of incense from a delicate chain, and the cloying scent of clove and sandalwood fills my nostrils and makes my eyes water.

"'Tis early for you to make your rounds, Father."

"Dame Galanta, we are here to take you to the holding cell."

I recoil and step backward. I've spent many a night locked in the tiny cell beside the catacombs. I have done nothing to warrant this.

"What offense have I given?"

"You are to be tried as a witch. We'll examine your body for the mark of Satan and when the witch hunter arrives from the mainland, you'll submit to his interrogation."

"I would know what I am being accused of, why I am being labeled a witch." I clench my teeth and fists to keep the quaver from my voice.

Father Mulcahy waves someone forward. The thatcher moves to the front.

"You did disobey the wishes of this man and entered his house. You carried evil spirits and ill humors that caused a death in his household. You were seen cavorting with fae at the Bealtaine festival. After you paid a visit to the cottage of the tavern maid, Rhona, her fever worsened and she died. And when you walked past fresh pails of milk on the Sabbath, it soured in your wake."

"You have cause to believe my daughter has aligned herself with Satan?"

"Aye."

My stepfather's expression tightens into a bland mask as he pivots toward me. "You must prove your innocence of these charges, Daughter. If they are warranted, I will not tolerate your presence in this god-fearing household and will condone whatever punishment is meted out to you."

My brothers suddenly loom in the street. "Is it true? Did you kill her?"

I shake my head in denial.

"We don't believe you. You are jealous of any woman who garners the attention of the men of the village because you will not. You are too skinny and too besmirched. And you reek of plants." He turns to the priest. "Take her. Her potions and possets are not welcome in our house."

Dougal's arms are crossed and he says nothing. Sometimes he is the only voice of reason amongst them. But not on this morning. And god-fearing household? The very thought of it threatens to send me into a fit of hysterical laughter.

One of the men steps forward, a thick length of rope unfurled in his hand.

"Cross your wrists for Elder Bream." The priest commands.

I obey because I have no choice. I lift my chin and do as he asks. I'm determined to bury my fear and camouflage my disdain.

The old man loops the rope around my crossed wrists, executes a swift slip knot, and pulls tight. He's made a leash of it, and he hands the end to my enemy.

The smile the priest aims in my direction is malicious. "Come along, Minion of Satan."

His sharp tug on the rope causes me to stumble forward. I barely catch myself and when I brush the tousled hair from my brow, his face is filled with malevolent intention.

I've long been aware of his loathing. But the hatred I see in his flat stare is more than that. Somehow I have come to symbolize all the things in this village beyond his control. He means to make an example of me. Both as a woman who challenges his authority by my refusal to be all that is meek and mild, and as a follower of the old ways.

Did someone spy me with Eachann at Bealtaine? Or are they simply making up tales to curry favor and garner attention? Surely if someone besides Mairead saw us, I would have had notice of their scrutiny before now.

They parade me through the streets like livestock headed for slaughter, and I'm bombarded by rotten vegetables and small stones as I hobble behind my accuser. He delights in swift jerks of the rope that make me careen toward the ground. I manage to catch myself with my hands, but my palms are bloodied by my efforts. My skin becomes ragged, bruised and marked by a thousand tiny cuts. I can feel the welts smarting from the dirt and pebbles lodged in them.

My stepfather's callous disregard and near condemnation hurts. He didn't protest at all. Not even half-heartedly. Instead, he foisted me on them with thinly veiled relief and a false obeisance that turns my stomach. I have felt the rod at his hands many times, but I have mastered the art of avoiding it. And he has intervened on my behalf with the priest, if only because he and my stepbrothers would starve without me.

But he has abandoned me. And so have many others. My gaze strays to many in the crowd of tormentors I once counted as friends. Their friendship was a falsehood, because they have joined those that jeer and cast stones. I wonder if Mairead would be standing with them too if she wasn't abed.

When I meet their stares, they look away. Like sheep, they have chosen to follow the path of least resistance. A hardened part of me wishes them ill for it. Without my healing skills, they will perish more swiftly. And with nothing but prayers to ease their path into darkness. If the priest decides to persecute more innocents in the name of his god, there will be no escape. These sheep will forsake the ways of their ancestors and deny all knowledge of simples or healing. Anything to preserve their lives.

Chapter Seventeen

Eachann

I've been waiting in the grove since dusk. The moon is high and will soon begin its descent in favor of the first light of dawn. There's no sign of her and she's sent no word. I fear the worst.

I know the death toll in the village from the new plague is steadily mounting. I have cautioned her against giving succor to those who will turn against her. I am certain they will throw her to the wolves if they are compelled to make a choice between her well-being and the approbation of the priest.

The turn of the season has brought nothing but hardship. There was no shower of blessings after Bealtaine and the harvest has suffered. The scant rainfall has hardened the earth, and the crops are puny and withered. The village is eager to blame someone. Who better to heap their woe on than a solitary girl who has never truly belonged? I fear the ire for the recent spate of malady and misfortune will fall on her shoulders.

My worry was wearing a path into the blanket of leaves when Callum's exasperated voice broke through the cycle of dread and despair.

"Let Carrig and I find out what has happened."

I've been pacing back and forth since their departure, fear of what has befallen her a knot in my stomach. When he finally tops the rise and strides toward me with a grim expression, I want to sink to the ground and curse the gods.

"They've taken her."

He nods tersely in agreement. "Before she even broke her fast. She spent the night at the bedside of one of the stricken against the wishes of the stepfather. The child died despite her ministrations, and she is being blamed. The priest is claiming she brought evil spirits into the house and showed Satan how to take the child's life."

I rake a hand down my face. "That's ludicrous. The child was likely beyond saving when they finally summoned her."

"Aye. But they're scared and looking for a scapegoat."

"Why are they holding her?"

"Ye know why, brother. 'Twas only a matter of time. She stands accused of witchcraft."

"On what evidence?"

"Soured milk, familiarity with evil spirits. And cavorting with one of the fae at Bealtaine. Someone spied the two of ye together. Is there more to the story, brother?"

I flush. I slipped past my self-proclaimed nursemaid that evening and made my way here alone. Because we had finally decided to fully give ourselves to each other and I wanted no interruptions. "I am not fae."

"No, we are not fae. But if someone saw you with her it is a mistake easily made. You are uncommonly tall and have that accursed mop of sunshine atop your head. Our kind call you the golden prince for a reason."

"We were cautious. We danced along the edges of the bonfire long after the celebration became nothing but drunken chaos. And we found peace and sanctuary in one of the hay byres on the heath."

"Sanctuary is what we're calling it now? You were noticed despite the drunken revelry. Or someone is spreading tales that have enough of a kernel of truth to be believable."

"She's done no wrong. All her efforts have been to help them instead of harm them."

"Their inquisition cares nothing for her intentions. Its sole purpose is to inflate the ego of the priest. They have summoned the witch hunter from the mainland."

"The one who tortures the accused and submits them to invasive examinations and impossible tasks?"

"The very one. You need to tell me now, Eachann, if he will find anything. Does she have any marks on her body that can be attributed to the touch of Satan?"

"She has an amber birthmark, shaped like spread wings, on her upper breast."

"How noticeable?"

I swallow as I remember tracing over every inch of it with my tongue. "They'll not miss it if they force her to disrobe."

"That does not bode well. It will be enough to confirm her guilt."

"We must rescue her from their clutches. Before it's too late." What if she doesn't survive their torture?

"Carrig and I will speak with Riordan. His network of spies and his skill at subterfuge will be useful. The four of us together will devise a plan."

"We don't have much time," I warn. "If they've summoned the witch hunter, we have a fortnight at most."

"Ye need to be prepared when we rescue her. She willnae be herself."

My nails dig into my palms. "She already bears the scars of their ignorance on her back. Hasn't she borne enough of their torment?"

My green girl is brave, but even the brave lose hope when it seems the whole world conspires against them and all those they thought were stalwart friends prove anything but.

"You need to be strong for her. An anchor. She'll have been beaten and starved. And possibly raped. Anything to force a confession from her – albeit a false one. Remember when we rescued Deirdru, her light was gone."

Last summer we rescued Carrig's sister from the Kraken Hold. She was kidnapped and tortured. Even after we rescued her and brought her home, she wasn't the same.

She was still stuck in that dark place. She stole the ceremonial dagger from the sheath that hangs in the throne room and took her own life. I will not let my wild one come to such a fate.

"Her spirit will be altered," I gruffly acknowledge.

"Aye. You will be the one mooring she hasn't lost."

"I'll be anything she needs me to be. And then I'll wreak my vengeance."

"If we slaughter her persecutors, they will demand vengeance."

"What benefit is having an army at my back if I cannot protect those I love? This is all the priest's doing. I'll strangle him with my bare hands and watch him choke on the saltwater filling his lungs. So he drowns from the inside out. And then I'll toss his body to the sharks."

"If you kill the priest you'll incite the rage of every village on these islands, and those all along the coast of the mainland. Are you determined to cause a war?"

"Don't tell me you're not looking forward to the prospect, brother. It's been at least two centuries since we defeated the mer kingdom to the east."

"These humans breed like a swarm of insects and devour or trample everything in their path. They far outnumber us and our battle skill may not prove enough. We do have disharmony in our own kingdom."

"There will always be disharmony."

"Not like this. One of my lieutenants advised me he overheard Cairneach and Creiddylad plotting to overthrow father."

"According to Father, they have been plotting his demise and their ascension to the throne for over a thousand years. Every attempt they've made has been foiled by their arrogance and incompetence."

"This time, they've sown dissent in the ranks as well. Father's continued refusal to trade with humans and his decision to ally ourselves to our nemesis are ensuring his popularity wanes."

"The alliance with the selkies may not happen if I balk at wedding their princess."

"There's no if, Brother. Yer devotion to this green witch is proof ye will balk at the arrangement Father has made. When will ye tell him?"

I sigh heavily. "I already have. I told mother first and she relayed my news to soften the blow of it. Father spoke to me himself last night. Though he believes this alliance is necessary to keep our kingdom intact, he understood why I must break the troth."

"Will he force me to carry through with yer obligation? Ye know I have no intention of settling down."

"I know you appreciate the attention you receive when you swing your sword. But mark me, your day of reckoning will come."

"I refuse to dwell on it. Especially since I've seen how pathetic falling love has rendered my brother."

I somber at his words. "If she perishes, a part of me will die at her side."

He clasps my forearm. "We'll do all we can to ensure that doesn't happen."

"That is your plan? I thought you were strategists!" I roar at my brother in disbelief.

"She is too closely guarded and placed in stocks under the beating sun, in full view of the entire village, for half the day."

"We cannot wait until after her trial. What if we are too late?"

"We must wait. There is no other way. If she is found guilty, we will cause a ruckus when they seek to burn her."

"What if we don't reach her in time?"

"Have faith, Brother. We will reach her. We have gone over every single detail of our plan again and again. We are only worried about her loyalty. I know ye've claimed she will remain steadfast no matter what befalls her, but what if they wear down her resolution?"

"I have no reason to question her love or loyalty."

"Just beware. Her allegiance may change under torture. What if she gives ye up to save herself? Her family professes itself Christian."

"She will not falter." I staunchly maintain. "She only wishes to be rid of that place."

"If she only seeks to escape, perhaps ye're no more than an expediency, Brother."

"I am not a means to an end. I would know. We have declared our vows. Even if they have not been sanctioned by the vizier or the kingdom."

Callum frowns. "Ye'd so recklessly violate the covenant we have with Lir? To only bind ourselves once our mate bears our sigil? If ye've acted prematurely, ye endanger the entire kingdom."

"I've violated no covenant. She is my true mate. I do not need a sigil ceremony to validate our union."

"I willnae be able to shield ye from Father's wrath and disappointment when he finds out ye've anticipated yer vows and planted yer seed."

"Father wants a grandson. And I already told Mother. I'm sure she relayed the news. He cares only that we find love and bear children to carry on his legacy."

"If that were all he cared about, he wouldn't have arranged the alliance with the selkies, even if he's allowing you to so recklessly sever it. Oh to be free from his dictates, like our sister."

Sabhinion is the first female offspring born to our clan in over seven centuries. The mating bond almost always results in sons, and those sons must find mortal mates to bear more sons. Sabh resents this because she thinks it's an archaic way to keep women from the line of succession.

"The true reason you doubt my sincerity is because you sense you are next. Your philandering ways will soon reach an end as mine have. Because Father will pressure you to take my place in his political maneuverings, whether the selkie girl is your mate or not."

"You think he'll expect me to cozen up to the selkie princess?"

"Once my intentions to renege on the match are made clear, yes. If they'll accept anyone other than the next in line for the throne."

He rubs his chin. "I've heard she's quite beautiful, if a bit fickle."

I lightly cuff his arm. "Not unlike you, little brother."

The fierce warlord blushes beneath his olive complexion. "I do nothing to encourage them."

"Whenever we have a tournament with the other kingdoms, the ground beneath your feet is littered with their favors. Are you certain you give them no encouragement? They vie for the privilege they think is your bed."

"The more aloof I am, the more determined they become. Many a night I am weary and want only rest. Only to find a naked woman reclining against my pillows."

I chuckle at his disgruntlement. "Once I am clearly unavailable, their efforts will only become more forward."

"I am becoming more and more reluctant to rescue your beleaguered bride to be."

I set aside my amusement. "No matter what comes, I appreciate everything you've done on my behalf."

"Ye're my brother, Eachann. As much as ye annoy me at times and make me want to toss ye into one of the caves, I am the only one permitted to feel that way. I have vowed to protect ye with my life – as my twin and my future king. If this green girl is yer life, I will protect her as well."

Callum is so stoic he rarely shows emotion. His confession and oath move me. "I hope your protection will be enough."

Chapter Eighteen

Galanta

They drag me into the village square. Just as they do every morning. I am numbed by endless days of torment and no longer protest.

"The witch hunter has arrived. Today he'll find the mark on your body we all know is there. And then I'll laugh while your flesh sizzles."

The thatcher's fetid breath skates over my face as he bends near. I struggle to maintain my composure, but inwardly shiver. My hands tremble and my spine is rigid with terror. I lift my chin to disguise my weakness. I will never let them see how their threats affect me.

"Bring the prisoner forward."

The crowd parts at the command, and I'm tugged through it. Hands pinch and prod me as we make our way to the front. My guard jerks the rope taut around my neck and I stumble forward. I am too weak to catch myself and I sprawl in the dirt.

I can't muster the strength to pull myself upright and kneel with my head hanging low. My hair is shorn. If they hadn't robbed me of it, it would be trailing on the ground.

I've given up all hope of salvation. It is too dangerous for my prince to intervene, and though it cleaves me in two, I understand his abandonment.

"Girl, you will stand for your examination."

The priest hauls me upright. The morning light slants across the visage of the witch hunter and I recoil. The flesh on one half of his face is covered in ridged scarring, his eye missing.

His delighted cackle rumbles through the clearing. "Your kind did this to me, little witch. It is why I will destroy every one of you."

He grabs the end of the leash from the priest. I tremble at the look in his eyes and resign myself to my fate. They will find the evidence they need to declare me a witch. Because the crowd is filled with bloodlust and needs someone to blame for their misfortunes.

"Strip her."

I close my eyes and drift far away. To a hay byre on the edge of night when a man they call a beast touched me with tenderness and professed his love.

The sough of wind glides over my naked skin, and then the pebbles rain down over me.

"Cease!" The hunter barks. "Her skin must be unblemished so I can spot her mark."

The crowd murmurs excitedly. The lechery crawls over me, stamping me in filth and shame. My hands are still bound, and I can't shield myself from it.

The rough pads of someone's fingers coast over my breasts and twist them in a bruising grip. When they glide over the slight mound of my stomach, I inhale.

"Not only is she marked with the favors of Lucifer, but she also carries his seed!"

He dips his head. "Witch, this bit of rock you wear around your neck will not protect you." He whispers in my ear and pinches my hip.

The shout of the priest has incited the crowd. The thump of their feet is restless, and I hear them jostling each other to surge forward for a closer look.

When I finally open my eyes, the priest is beaming triumphantly. The witch hunter has a smirk on his ruined face.

"What is my fate to be?" I wish my hands were unbound. I would cradle my stomach. "You cannot condemn an innocent child to my fate."

"You'll burn at the stake a fortnight hence. On the Sabbath. And that is no child. You are unwed. You bear the mark of one of Lucifer's minions, and you carry his demon spawn." The priest turns to the hunter for confirmation.

"Aye. She'll burn at the stake on the Sabbath two weeks hence. A fitting time to purge this village of its wickedness."

Someone tosses a blanket over my nakedness, and I numbly submit when they herd me toward my captivity. Every step back I am pelted by stones. I barely feel them raining down on my head and shoulders. My dreams of fire and destruction were a premonition of this.

I've eaten nothing but a midday cup of thin gruel for weeks now. The taste is bitter, but I must do all I can to keep up what little strength I have. My cell is weathered gray stone with no windows. It is bleak and the scrabbling mice are my only company. I shiver in the dank cold every night. They took the blanket away from me as soon as we reached the church and thrust me in here with only my threadbare shift.

The evenings slide seamlessly into each other. My lips and throat are raw from lack of water. The babe is alive but moves more sluggishly with each passing day.

The scuffling of boots rouses me from my reverie. I lift my head to find the witch hunter. His hands are wrapped around the bars of my cell and he's leering down at me.

"I have a bargain for ye, witch."

His intent is unmistakable. I can only imagine what his bargain entails and swallow my revulsion at the thought of him between my legs. "I am not interested in bargains."

"So haughty now," he sneers. "Ye won't be so high and mighty when you feel the flames. I'd take you as my servant to instruct in the true religion. To serve as an example of the beneficence of the church. A reminder that those who have committed grievous sins can earn forgiveness."

"Your servant? Someone to mend your clothes and cook your meals? Or something more? Speak plainly, witch hunter."

"A cook travels with me to attend to my particular diet. And I have a manservant who keeps my raiment spotless. I need a leman, a companion."

"So you'd make the woman you have called the devil's whore your own?"

"Making this concession is an honor you do not deserve,"

"It is not an honor. It is insult."

When my spittle lands just shy of his boots he laughs. "Oh, I would enjoy bringing you to heel, witch. Mayhap I'll convince the priest that I've had a change of heart and I believe you're redeemable after all."

My heart stills in my chest. To be bound to this man who is truly a monster? He hides it behind a mask, but he is nothing more than a slithering serpent. Eachann would gladly gut him.

"I have no need of redemption. If your god is as omniscient and merciful as you claim, he knows who is deserving of what."

"You would refuse my offer of salvation?"

"Wholeheartedly."

"You will let your child burn with you?"

"Rather than submitting to you instead? Yes."

"You are just a whore with a talent for herbs. Like all the other women I have condemned. But you are the most beautiful sinner, and so I am willing to be lenient."

"I will soon be in no condition to play the whore for anyone, fire or not."

"I have no reservations about plowing a furrow another man has planted seed in. And I know it was a man, and not Satan. The Lord of Darkness has his sights set on things other than whatever calamities have befallen these islands."

"My answer is still no."

"You have four days to change your mind and save yourself and the babe. Do not be foolish. Whoever the father is, he has clearly abandoned you to your fate."

I turn my head to the wall and ignore his retreat.

Has he truly abandoned me? How could he know of my fate? I have no means of summoning the ravens and they are the only way I have of getting word to him. Rescue seems an impossibility, but I dream of it nonetheless.

Chapter Nineteen

Eachann

My father has been accommodating in the face of my defection. But he still demands my presence here at his side. I've spent the day settling frivolous disputes. Every whining complaint put before me is another spike designed to inflame my temper. When my aunt and uncle step forward to plead an interruption in the succession the last thread of control I have slips away. They make this demand to declare their right to the next ascension every moontide. It is only one of the many ways they flaunt and challenge the authority of the throne.

I rise from my chair and step down to their level. "What makes you think you are fit to lead this kingdom? Your skill with weapons is abysmal, your diplomacy leaves much to be desired, and you do not know the meaning of the word sacrifice."

Cairneach sneers. "You are one to talk of being fit, prince. You do not cut the same figure on the battlefield your brother does. We all know you would rather sequester yourself with your harp than pick up a sword. You cannot truly expect to solve every conflict with music."

I flush. "The bards of old used music to soothe tempers and garner accord."

"Accord like that you have garnered with the selkie kingdom."

My astonishment must be clearly writ, because he leans closer. "Ah yes, nephew, I know of your broken betrothal. Do not speak to me of sacrifice. You know nothing of it or what it entails. You blindly follow the lead of your cock instead."

Is this what the entire court secretly believes? Has my father shielded me from their disdain until now? "I follow where my beast leads me, not my cock. And my beast led me to my mate. Just as your king was led to his. Denying the sanctity of that bond in favor of a political alliance is spitting in the eye of the gods. For they are the ones to bestow such a gift."

His mouth flops open and I unbind my hair in response. He knows what this means. It means I will unleash my power against him if he challenges me further. His mouth snaps shut and the glares he and his wife level in my direction are sharp enough to lance the most stubborn of boils.

I curtly bow in the direction of the central throne. "Father, I must see to the welfare of my mate."

I told my mother of Galanta's capture, and from my father's grim reaction and terse nod, I know she relayed my story. He placed a high enough value on his love for her that he cannot expect me to stand idly by while the woman I love needs my protection. The lines around his mouth soften and he subtly nods. "Go, my son. And take your brother with you."

I've heard nothing from Riordan or his men on the outcome of her trial. I can do nothing on her behalf here, and it is the last place I want to be right now.

I stride from the hall without glancing back. Callum and Carrig fall in behind me. All three of us are silent as we dive into the sea. Taking our each uisge form, and cleaving the water with our hooves, will reach her faster than rowing a tiny boat.

I'm the first ashore. As soon as I shake the water from my mane, smoke fills my nostrils. The center of the village is just beyond the harbor, and the jeering crowd mulls about. I instinctively know she is the object of their derision. I let the swift thunder of my hooves, and the flash of my teeth cleave a path through the spectators. I see the flash of Carrig and Callum's swords and know they have transformed back into their human forms and will protect my flank.

I barely reach her in time. The flames already snap and crackle at the hem of her skirts.

I furiously stamp them out and let the saltwater rise in my veins to finish the task. One strike of my hoof douses the flames. I follow the lead of my brother and transform so I can use my dirk to slash the ropes that bind her.

She is silent and unmoving. Even after I have released her. When I lift her into my arms, she is brittle. She has found an inner sanctuary I cannot breach and I brace myself for the struggle to come. Callum warned I would be her only mooring. I see the truth of it now and the music welling inside me holds the mournful, somber notes of a dirge.

I thought I knew the weight and warmth of her. I knew those things when she was whole in my arms. She is far from whole now. The grimy figure I am cradling against my chest is not my wild heart. She is beaten and broken. Both of her eyes are nearly swollen shut, and her face is a mass of bruises. The imprint of a boot mars her upper cheek, and both her jaw and nose are askew. She moans in pain when I shift my stance and I fear she has broken ribs as well.

The hard mound of her stomach still presses between us. I know she did everything she could to protect the babe. I shudder at the thought of what sacrifices were required of her.

When I turn to face her tormentors, they are scurrying away in terror. Callum and Carrig stand back-to-back, their blades slicing through the air with deadly precision.

"I am transforming again so I can get her to safety," I shout above the melee.

"We are nearly finished here." Callum's chest barely heaves from the effort of terrorizing her accusers. "How will you get her to safety?"

I was so intent on her salvation I didn't consider all the details. "Can we use the ropes that bound her to fashion a bridle and tie her to me?"

"Aye. We'll ensure the knots are secure."

"Where will you take her?" Carrig asks.

"Mother and Father may be ready to accept my decision, but the kingdom is not. I will take her to the keep on the headland."

"I know you are restoring it, but it's far from ready. The only thing still standing there is the old watchtower."

"I can care for her there and watch for our enemies at the same time."

Carrig gives me a sharp nod. "We will stand sentry as well. And I will fetch Sabhinion to physick her."

I hand my bride to Carrig and let my beast rise once again. Callum swiftly fashions a makeshift bridle. My beast has never worn one, and tosses his head in displeasure. He finally settles and grudgingly accepts the restraint. I can sense his acquiescence is solely because he is as worried for her as I am.

When Carrig sets her on my back, she is the lightest burden I've ever carried. She still hasn't uttered a word, and her limbs are stiff when Callum lashes them to my neck. I will avenge their treatment of her.

I dive into the water, desperate to get her as far away from this place as I can. Twice, I almost lose her to the waves. It is only the latch of my teeth on her tunic that keeps her from being swept away.

When we finally reach the headland, I don't bother to retrieve the cache of clothing I keep stowed there. She is all that matters. She has regained some awareness, because she shifts in my arms. She lays her hand on my cheek and it is colder than the deepest seawater. "Mo stoirm," she murmurs. She smiles faintly and closes her eyes again. I kiss each lid and hoist her higher in my arms, nearer the solid beat of my heart.

"Sabh!" I bellow in desperation. My mate's pulse is shallow and thready, and each breath shudders in her chest. The heat from the pyre blistered her feet and legs.

My sister meets me at the gate and swings it open. "I have made up a bed and gathered the medicines I will need to treat her. I had to consult with Aunt Arie, because mortal constitutions are unlike ours."

"I thank you sister. I have never seen her so frail."

"They've beaten and starved her. And likely raped her. She'll need time to heal before she'll be ready for the sigil ceremony that will be required. Father has decreed you've flouted enough tradition and must at least abide by that one. She'll be unwelcome at the keep until it's done."

"I know Father's tolerance can only be stretched so far. And he can't afford to be lenient with so much unrest."

Our uncle's temper tantrum during today's hearings is only the most recent show of rebellion. As more and more ships ply trade with the villages, our subjects clamor for access to those riches. My father has denied it. He does not want us to become dependent on foreign luxuries or mortal bargains.

Cairneach has made it known far and wide that his reign would allow such access. He claims that no longer having to spin our own cloth or brew our own mead will leave the court time to indulge in more pleasurable activities. Father has said he will not allow his kingdom to become one of debauchery and corruption like that of Caesar. He claims there is a reason he and my grandfather fought against the Roman invasion.

The only concession he made to their influence was the installation of baths at the keep. They are supplied by the hot water that boils from the earth.

When I set my mate upon the bed, she refuses to let go. She doesn't stir, but I catch a fleeting glimpse of her dimple. I settle myself alongside her and she curls her body into mine. I lend her my warmth as Sabh removes her tattered gown and gently sponges her upper body clean.

My sister applies salve to her bruised face and lathers linens with it before she wraps her blistered legs. When she finishes her ministrations, her gaze is troubled.

"What is it, sister?"

"She will heal physically, I am certain of it. But she has deeper wounds we cannot treat. She will be forced to pull herself from the brink. To be strong for your child."

"I ken what she has been through." The tears clog my throat and my sister kneels beside me.

"I know you do, brother. You must be mindful that it is different for women. She may recoil at your intimate touch. Now she is nestled against you because you are safe and warm. When she wakes, she may not be as accommodating."

"I will erase their touch from her body the only way I know how. With blood and vengeance. And if she never lets me touch her again in that way, I will understand. I will accept it and remain true. I should have taken her with me despite her protests to the contrary. I would have overcome her misgivings. But my hesitancy led her to this state, and I will never forgive myself."

Sabh lays her hand on my forearm. "Eachann, this is not your fault. There is no one to blame but the priest and the witch hunter. They stirred the village to a frenzy and stoked the flames of boredom and discontent."

"The priest and the hunter will pay for what they have done. The forfeit for their part in this will be their lives."

"I know you are angry. But remember we cannot afford to make more enemies."

"They are already our enemies, sister. Though they have yet to assault us, the time for it draws near. I have seen what little respect they have for those who do not follow their god."

"You both should sleep. 'Twill give you time to weigh the wisdom of your actions, brother. You cannot act rashly."

She stands and adds more peat to the hearth. "There is bread and cheese in the crock on the table. Feed her when she wakes."

When she softly shuts the door, I turn back to the precious bundle in my arms. Despite my sister's warnings, I cannot let the attack on my mate go unanswered. Not only for her sake, but for the sake of all the innocents these men will torture if their arrogance remains unchecked and their appetite for power is allowed to grow unrestrained.

I left my mate in the care of my sister. She still hasn't acknowledged me, and turned aside, her hands white-knuckled around the curve of her stomach when I bent to kiss her farewell. I've told only Callum of my intentions, and he insisted on accompanying me. I doubt I'll need his assistance but welcome it all the same.

I have two targets. The priest and the witch hunter. Riordan and his network have kept abreast of their whereabouts, and I know precisely where to find them.

The village is eerily quiet when we land at the wharf. There is scant light from the new moon and none of the cottages have lit candles. We wade ashore, transform into our human form, and skulk through the shadows until we reach the chapel.

The priest is on his knees when we fling open the doors. He is on his knees, but he is not praying.

His mouth is wrapped around the cock of the witch hunter.

They spring apart at our approach. The priest swipes his hand across his mouth and the hunter crosses his arms over his chest, his ruddy member glistening with spittle in the candlelight. The sight disgusts me – not because of what they do. All of we each uisge are adventurous and have taken lovers from all species and genders. They disgust me because they had the temerity to berate my chosen bride for something they secretly indulge in. Our culture reviles hypocrisy, and this is one of the most hypocritical acts I've ever encountered.

I step closer and the priest whirls around at the drag of my feet across the floor. He stumbles back, flailing. His foot catches on the hem of his robe and he goes down in a pile of skinny legs and fabric.

My laughter echoes between us. "Why do you cower, priest?"

"My God will protect me from your evil. I do not cower in fear."

"Your God will not protect you from my anger or my retribution. How dare you drag my mate through your muddy streets? How dare you chain her in your prison? How dare you light a pyre beneath her?"

"We dared because she is evil. The hand of Satan has lain over her brow and she has been a willing vessel for his demon seed. You are one of his minions as well."

The witch hunter tucks himself back into his trews as he makes his pronouncement.

I shudder at what might have happened. I remember the heat of the flames on my hooves as I dowsed them with saltwater, and how fragile she felt when I dropped to my knees and scooped her into my arms.

She clung to me, her breath hot and shallow as she burrowed closer. Her hands were like claws around my neck and she was shivering and sobbing.

"What gives you the right to punish?"

"I am the voice of God, and he gives me that right."

These men are supremely confident of their divine right to dispense justice.

"He gives you the right to torture the innocent? To exert your position of power over those who cannot retaliate?"

"I have the blessing of my lord and savior and am called to make light from darkness. A deep evil festers here, the product of false idols and hellish beasts."

"Galanta is hardly more than a girl – she is not a scion of wickedness."

"You are wicked yourself, prince. Together, you are an appalling abomination. The world should not suffer the fruit of your union."

"Her power is of the earth – what is more sacred than that? Her power is in healing and new growth, not of doom and death." Her magic may be stronger than that of the tides, and the only force that can withstand the darkness the seers have foretold.

"The earth's power stinks of witch's blood. Of concoctions and remedies that cause more harm than good. Of paths righteous people have forsaken."

"Her path is the oldest path – ordained and sanctified by the Goddess herself."

"There is no goddess. Only the one true god I serve."

"Your god will never have full dominion over the earth. His servants are intolerant and cruel, and spread his word through fearmongering and persecution instead of kindness and forbearance."

The witch hunter cackles. "The rule of your kind is nearing its end, prince. And there is nothing you can do to stop it. The tides are their own wheel of time, and every ebb and flow diminishes the power of the each uisge."

"Your palaver grows tiresome." Before Callum can intervene, I slash his throat and silence his poison forever. His body falls and as the severed head rolls across the stone floor, the priest scrabbles away. I have no more patience. I launch my dirk at his back and it impales the base of his neck. He gurgles once before he collapses, toppling the candelabra. The flames catch on his robe and the oil from the spilt incense ignites.

"What should we do?"

"Let it burn."

When we step into the water, the village is rousing itself from slumber and shouting for buckets.

Chapter Twenty

Galanta

I remember the heat of the flames beneath my feet. I remember the crack of my ribs as the witch hunter kicked me while I lay on the floor of my cell. I remember the cuff to my jaw from the thatcher that sent me careening into the stone wall. I remember how alone I was. How dark and cold and blighted of hope. I can barely make out the glimmer of light and movement through the bruising that covers my eyes.

I think my rescuer has returned and I want to express my gratitude. But the words stick in my throat like rocks. From lack of water and malicious hands and fear that I still dream in the dank and dread that encompassed my world.

"They are dead at my hands. Gone forever. They will never touch you again."

My eyes fill with tears, and he drops to his haunches in front of me. When he strokes the sweaty curls away from my brow, I tense beneath his touch. I know he would never hurt me, but even his gentle caress stirs foul memories. "Love." I manage to croak past my smoke damaged vocal chords.

"And you are my love. Everything I do - it is all for you. Even if you are not ready to accept it. You have my sword and my shield, my unwavering loyalty and the wild heart of my beast." He unfurls the hand curled beneath my chin and places it over his heart. "You will always have these things."

When I wake again, he is gone. A woman who looks to be my age is bent over the hearth.

She turns when I stir beneath the blankets. "You're finally awake."

I struggle to sit upright, and she comes to my side. Once she's helped me and situated the pillows to her satisfaction, she takes my hands in hers. "I am Sabhinion and I have always wanted a sister. My brothers have resisted mating for so long, I never thought I would have one. Yet here you are. Eachann's chosen bride."

"Where is he?"

Her gaze falters and she looks away. "He and my father are meeting with the selkie queen and her emissary."

"You seem unsure of the outcome."

"She is not an easy woman to negotiate with and I fear what sort of compensation she will demand for the broken troth."

"Surely not someone's life?"

"Nothing so harsh as that. But likely half our coffers. And I know my father worries they will not be enough to tide us over. At the behest of the church, more and more of the villages refuse our trade. The creatures of the sea are our brethren, and we abstain from consuming them when we can."

"Callum cannot serve in Eachann's stead?"

"Even if he were willing, which he is not, she considers her daughter too far above a second son. It is too far away from the throne for her liking."

"Only gold will appease her? There must be something I can do considering this is my fault."

"You are not to blame. There is nothing you can do to appease her. The sight of you would certainly enrage her. She was confident she had my brother trussed up and ready to serve on a platter to her daughter."

"Eachann is not the sort of man to consent to being trussed up."

"No, he isn't. None of the each uisge men are. My brothers and their best friend least of all."

Her expression turns wistful at the end of her pronouncement. Finding out why will be a welcome distraction from my chaotic thoughts of her brother. "You have feelings for him?"

She narrows her gaze. "Who?"

"Their best friend."

She sighs and flops onto the mattress beside me. "Little good it does me. Carrig barely acknowledges my existence. I'm certain he sees me as naught but an annoying pest."

"Perhaps you have misread his perception of you?"

She wags her head with a desolate expression. "Nay. I once tried to steal a kiss as he was emerging from his bath.

He snatched the towel around his waist and told me I had no business propositioning him."

"How long ago did it happen?"

"Three hundred years ago. He hasn't met my gaze since."

"Do Eachann and Callum know?"

She groans and covers her face. "They tease me mercilessly."

"He cannot be that oblivious to you. Mayhap he snatched the towel from embarrassment, not annoyance."

"Do not give me false hope, new sister. My brothers constantly warn I'll never receive a kiss if I keep my head buried in books."

"Learning is naught to scoff at."

"I tend to spout obscure facts when my nerves assail me. All three of them grimace when I do it and turn away."

"Mayhap you should spout poetry instead."

"That would be more amusing to them than facts. But most of the poems in our collection are odes to love. I couldn't recite them and not address the object of my affection."

"We shall craft another strategy to catch his attention."

Aiding my new sister-in-law in this endeavor will strengthen our bond.

She leaps from the bed so quickly she nearly loses her footing. "Rest easy, Galanta. I shall begin making notes so we may consider them tomorrow."

I smile drowsily. Her enthusiasm and ready acceptance have eased my fear of belonging here. "Tomorrow then," I murmur as I let sleep pull me under once again.

I bolt upright in the bed, and the only light is from a single candle that rests on a ledge. "You are safe," a voice murmurs beside me.

It is him. "I know."

"Your throat is healing."

"Yes," I whisper in agreement as I lie back down.

I'm suddenly aware of the heat of his limbs wrapped around my body and I can't withhold my reaction. My spine and shoulders stiffen.

He sighs mightily and lifts himself away from me. "I am sorry. I meant no harm. I could see our babe moving in your womb and wanted to feel it too."

I turn to face him and grab one of his hands between my own. "I will bear it," I tell him as I place it on the mound of my stomach.

His face creases in a gentle smile and he closes his eyes. His expression is one of serenity and quiet joy. Seeing it is well worth the price of my discomfort.

He opens his eyes and lifts his other hand to my face. He leans forward, cradling my jaw, and brushes my forehead with his lips. "I have missed you, mo chridhe fiadhaich."

I bite my lip before bending over him to return the gesture. Another smile suffuses his face. "I missed you as well. I am sorry I lost hope."

He raises his hand again but drops it just as suddenly. "Do not apologize for your doubts, leannan. Those doubts were warranted. You have never had anyone to lean on, and a lifetime of isolation and disappointment are not so easily forgotten. I wanted to rescue you as soon as I learned of your capture."

"You couldn't do it then. I was too closely guarded."

"That is what Callum told me. He cautioned me against insurmountable odds and the repercussions of acting so rashly. He, Carrig and Riordan assured me that waiting until the last possible moment, when the village was distracted, was our best chance."

"When your beast came to my rescue, I thought I was dreaming."

"I had to tie you to my back." He rubs his thumb over my wrists. "The sea churned with anger that day, and our journey was so perilous I nearly lost you to it."

"You were the last thing I thought of before I felt the heat beneath my feet and closed my eyes."

"What were your thoughts of me?"

"I was sorrowful on your behalf. That you wouldn't have the chance to know your son."

"My parents know of the babe, but we must hide your condition from the court."

"Why?"

"Anticipating my vows will be seen as a reckless act of rebellion. We are forbidden from spilling our seed in a woman unless she bears our sigil."

"What's the sigil like?"

He raises my hand to his mouth and places a kiss in the middle of my palm before curling my fingers around it. "The sigil is two runes. The first one is the symbol of the house of Lir. The second one is the secret name of my beast. I will carve them both on your wrist and cover the wound with my cuff." He taps the leather band on his upper arm. "Once I give you my runes, you use the dagger to carve a sigil as well. You'll inscribe the rune of binding just above my heart. It will forever tame my beast and fulfill our bond."

"Why must rituals always be steeped in blood?"

"Is that a rhetorical question, my love?"

"Yea. I know why it is so. Blood is the most sacred exchange because it is imbued with life."

"Our ceremony will wait until you are healed."

It will be several weeks before the bruises fade completely, the blistering is covered by new skin, and the bones are healed. I don't know how long it will be before the invisible wounds fade enough to be borne.

Chapter Twenty-One

Eachann

"I demand restitution for the dishonor against me and my kingdom."

"My son and your daughter have exchanged no betrothal gifts. There was no formal agreement."

"You would go back on your word, King Bhaltair?"

"There is no word to go back on. We were still negotiating our bargain. Even you would agree that your daughter deserves more than to be bound to someone who has clearly lost their heart to someone else."

"Queen Iolanthe."

She whirls to face me. "What do you have to say for yourself, Prince?"

"I fully intended to honor whatever agreement you and my father reached. But the woman I love will soon bear my child."

She reels back. "Abomination!"

The crowd of courtiers surrounding her echoes her cry. My father's expression is thunderous.

"Silence!" He roars.

The cacophony comes to an abrupt halt. The king rarely shows his anger.

"I have heard my son's petition and granted it. Though he has anticipated his vows, it is clear this woman is his mate and the gods approve of their union."

"He has frivolously cast aside generations of tradition to satisfy his lust." One of the brehons observes.

I clench my fists and rise to my feet. "There was no frivolity in my decision."

"Sit down, Prince," my father admonishes before turning to the crowd again. "Traditions change. There was a time when the sigil ceremony did not exist. When the words a couple exchanged were enough. My son has promised to honor our tradition when his bride is fully healed."

"How is she afflicted? Does her presence here endanger us all?"

My Aunt Creiddylad's sly interjection sends the crowd spiraling into chaos again.

My father raises a hand to quiet it. "She has wounds she must recover from. Her presence here endangers no one."

"You allow your son to throw aside my daughter for a woman who isn't even whole?"

My father glares back at the queen. "As I have informed you, my son is not throwing aside your daughter. We have executed no settlement agreements."

"I repeat. I demand retribution for this abysmal treatment of my family and my kingdom."

The queen is grandstanding, but there are murmurs of agreement from the crowd.

"We will come to an agreement in the privacy of the royal council room. Not here."

"My daughter will accompany me as whatever we decide will determine her fate." She waves a hand and a slender selkie maiden steps forward. She wears no jewels, and her frock isn't embellished like that of her mother.

She dips into a curtsey, and I respond with a nod. A wry smile curves her mouth. "I can speak for myself, mother."

She steps in front of the dais and clasps her hands in front of her. "I have no desire to wed or bear children. I want to be a scholar, not a nursemaid."

The queen yanks the girl to her side. "Disregard her pronouncement. This alliance may not be her choice, but it is her duty."

"Regardless, this discussion will take place in my council chambers between the two of us. Ruler to ruler. Our children need not attend and will be refused entry."

My father's tone brooks no argument and when he rises and sweeps from his throne, the queen accompanies him.

I'm watching their departure when there is a tap on my elbow. When I turn, the selkie princess is standing at my side. "If you hadn't cried off, I would have been forced to run away."

"You are so averse to marriage?"

"Yes. If it is only an instrument for procreation."

"You don't believe we would have come to hold affection for each other?"

"As good friends, perhaps. But my heart is held by another."

"You have found happiness with someone else as well? Your true mate?"

"Yes, I believe she is my soulmate. My mother will never condone our union as it is anathema to everything she believes in. She would not consider my commitment an appropriate preservation of her legacy."

"Because you love another female?"

She shrugs. "That is not what is uncommon and abhorrent to my mother. It is my willingness to forsake all others for Saoirse."

This pale, scholarly princess has more wisdom and empathy in the crook of her smallest finger than her mother does in her entire frame. "That is how I feel about Galanta. Luckily, my father respects my devotion. Even though there are obstacles to it."

"Would that my mother was so tolerant."

"You have no other siblings she can manipulate?"

"My two brothers were ambushed and killed on Soag two moons ago."

"Why is their demise not common knowledge?"

"She doesn't want the rest of the kingdoms to know how tenuous her reign is, or that the future of the court hangs in such precarious balance."

"She'll not be able to hide it for much longer."

"Don't underestimate her. She's a master of deception."

"You think she will seek to ally herself with another nation?"

"That is exactly what she will do. Be on your guard, prince, for her treachery. I have learned to be."

She bows her head and whirls on her heel. I am torn between the need to warn my father of the queen's duplicity and the need to seek out my mate.

The desire to see my mate and assure her well-being wins out over my loyalty to my father. I cannot interrupt his counsel without arousing suspicion. I will share it with him once the queen and her party have left our shores.

My mate is curled on her side, eyes fluttering in slumber, when I reach the keep. Though it is midday, I find myself in need of rest as well. I curl my arms around her and close my eyes.

When we wake, it is dusk. We have missed the evening meal, and her eyes light up like they always do when I present her with cheese to assuage her hunger. At least that hasn't changed.

"I know it is dangerous, but there is something I need to retrieve from the grove."

"I can get it for you."

"No. It is more dangerous for you. You have slain my enemies. If you deposit me on the far side of the island I can get to the grove without being seen."

"When?"

"In two days' time, when the moon is full. No one uses the cove. There are too many rocks for them to safely navigate it. You can retrieve me there just before dawn."

"And that will be the last time you set foot in that cursed place?"

She leans forward and brushes her thumb over the curve of my cheek. "I vow it is the last time we'll be separated."

I hold her hand there. "That is all I want."

Chapter Twenty-Two

Galanta

I have lain about for a fortnight. The babe makes its presence known, and Eachann fell asleep last night with his arm curved around my waist and his head resting against my stomach.

He's been trying to convince me to allow one of his guard to retrieve the grimoire. I've refused every single time because this is the legacy of my family. It will be the legacy of our bairn. I cannot trust it to someone else. I am afraid to uncover it, but I am more afraid I will need those mysteries and that power to protect my mate and our child.

He insists on accompanying me all the way to the grove and is reluctant to leave me here alone. "Leannan, I will stay with you while you retrieve it."

"No. I must do this alone. The book holds too much earth magic. It will be hostile to your presence and I may have to subdue it. I refuse to endanger you."

"I will be well out of the way. Let me stay. Callum and my guard can retrieve us both." He sighs heavily and begins pacing back and forth.

"Mo stoirm, you have duties you need to attend to. And I would not have you come to any harm. I am strong enough for this and no one knows of my return or your presence here. I will see you at dusk."

He clasps my hand and pulls me against him. "The sea is angry today. Like it is trying to warn me of what is to come."

I brush the tendrils of hair from his cheeks. "The sea is angry because it is the season of storms. That is all." I lift to my toes and place a gentle kiss on the grim line of his lips. "Be easy, mo stoirm. It is only your fear, and it is unwarranted."

His hold on my waist tightens and his lips land on mine. The kiss is designed to slip beneath my resolve. It is both tender and fierce.

"I am afraid to let you go, mo chridhe faidhaich," he murmurs.

"You must. But only for now. This is for us. For our bairn."

He steps away, but catches my hands. "I will be at the cove when the sun begins sinking toward its journey west. Be careful, leannan, for you carry my heart." He lets go, one finger at a time, raising each to his mouth and placing a gentle kiss on the knuckle. When he kisses the last one, he gives me a deep bow and turns on his heel.

I watch him go. The wind is rising, and it snags his hair loose from its bindings, so it whips in the breeze like golden flames.

I want to follow him and tell him nothing matters more than protecting our growing family, and that the book can molder for an eternity beneath the leaves and dirt.

But I cannot afford to abandon the legacy of my ancestors, especially now I will have the chance to add to the knowledge stored between its pages.

I must say my farewells to the grove and the spirits that haunt it. My mother only visits me in dreams now, and I feel the last of her presence slipping away as I ready myself for a future I never imagined. Her last warning to me, that my saltwater prince would bring me nothing but pian and sorrow, echoes in my head.

I will need whatever incantations and eldritch magic are in the book. Whatever guidance and protection it can provide.

I place my hand against the oak that is the grandfather of every tree in the grove. The sap rises beneath my palm, and I feel its call in my blood. Just as I bow my head, something rustles in the trees behind me.

"Who is there?"

Have I somehow roused the eldritch king from his slumber? "Show yourself."

I have a dagger in the belt at my waist. I brandish it at the empty air. "I am armed. Come no closer."

My stomach roils again. This time not only from fear. Noxious bile rises in my throat as I fall to my knees, still clutching the dagger.

I feel the trickle of wetness between my legs and when I raise my skirt, my thighs are spotted with blood.

Something foul roils in my stomach, and I fear my captors will seek to purge me of the babe. I barely make it to the grove, and collapse on the bed of leaves.

The roiling is now a stabbing pain and I cannot rise. I will crawl if I must. The spell book cannot remain here. It is the legacy of my family and irreplaceable.

I raise myself to my knees and crawl to the foot of the rowan where I buried it seven years ago.

I have nothing to uncover it, so I scrabble in the dirt until my hands are caked and my nails are broken and jagged.

When I finally uncover it, the oilskin I wrapped it in crumbles at my touch. The grimoire inside is fragile, but intact. I sigh in relief. When I brush my hand over the pages, the crystal swinging from my neck flares in response.

I'm wrapping the tome for the journey when the pain strikes again. This time it radiates outward from my womb, numbing my limbs. Whatever poison they used was meant to cause sheer agony. My body convulses on the ground, and blood fills my mouth because I've bitten my tongue. The grove fades around me.

There are lead weights on my eyelids, and I struggle to open them.

The familiar walls of our cottage greet me. I'm lying on a pallet in front of the cold dead hearth. I recognize nothing.

I stumble to my feet; my skirts soaked in blood and bundle the sheets in my arms.

The door crashes open and my stepbrothers and stepfather stride through it.

"We could not allow you to escape. Your demon lover deserved to burn in the fires of hell."

"What have you..." I don't finish the sentence. I feel myself falling again. The cottage disappears. Just as the grove did. A huge bower constructed from willow and wild rose rises before me. Golden orbs float around the edges, and a hooded figure with a raven on each shoulder steps in front of me.

"Why can you not let me die as I wish? My babe is gone. My love is gone."

"The women of your family are bound to me. It is your eternal duty to serve me. You will become one of my ravens for a time, ferrying the souls killed in battle back to this plane. In exchange for your life, you will serve as one of my winged couriers."

I have no wish to serve this goddess. "I choose to die."

"This is not the end of your story, foolish lass. My sisters tell me you are meant for much more. The choice is not in your hands."

"Have I not borne enough?"

"The strong are given only what their spirit can withstand. And your spirit is forged of my wildness and fury. You are battered but unbroken."

"I feel broken and weary."

"Your body was slowly poisoned by your jailers. They would not suffer a servant of the old ones to live. You have not only lost your babe. You have lost your mate. They have destroyed him, and as one of my ravens you will have the chance to exact no small measure of revenge."

I want the darkness of the Lord of Death to envelop me as I claim his sweet bliss. My life has been naught but pain and struggle.

"Your prince is not dead as your kind perceives death. His spirit ravages the shoreline even now. You must go with my maidens now to retrieve his body and ensure it has the berth it needs for restoration. So he will be prepared for his ascension when you have the knowledge and power to restore him to this plane."

She beckons two of her maidens forward and they lift me to my feet. Their hands are icy manacles on my wrists, holding the stark desperation of deep winter. They cleanse me of the blood that marks my loss. I am numb with the burden of the ruination I have wrought, and quietly submit to their ministrations.

Chapter Twenty-Three

Eachann

My mate isn't waiting for me when we land. Instead, we are met with a bristling hedge of swords. My uncle stands in the middle of it, his shoulders thrown back and his mouth curved in a smug smile. Two of his men tug my bound father forward.

I never thought she would betray me. She arranged the time and place of our landing and was the only human aware of the details.

I'm surrounded as soon as I fully emerge from the water. My struggle against them is half-hearted because nothing is sacred if she has forsaken me. I fling two attackers from my back but cannot escape the man that wrests my sword from my grasp. I have nothing but teeth and hooves, and I need the taste of blood before I can transform again. I am hemmed in on all sides, and I howl in pain when there is a vicious kick to my lower spine. I stumble forward, barely upright and someone slashes my exposed ribs.

Callum is shouting directions, but the sound of the surf is pounding in my ears and I can't make out what he's telling me.

I pull my dirk from the belt at my waist, but it is a paltry defense against their broadswords. I feint left and right as I back toward the water. If I can make it to the waves, I can summon help to my side. The creatures that dwell in the depths will come to my aid if I agree to give them a future boon.

The water laps against my heels, and I open my mouth to call on a school of whales.

The sound never makes it out of my mouth. The hilt of a knife quivers from my heart, and as I fall to my knees, another one severs my jugular.

The world fades as the words faded in my throat. My limbs are numb and I sink into the darkness. The last thing I hear is my brother's anguished protest.

My spirit will not let go. Something or someone tethers it here and I hover above the melee. If it is my love for her and she is alive, I will haunt her to the end of her days. I watch in horror as my uncle and his wife slit my father's throat and drop his limp body onto the sand. My mother will sense his death and if Callum doesn't reach her in time, she will take her own life. And if he doesn't rescue Sabh, Cairneach will imprison her until she marries our cousin Mordecainn.

There is nothing I can do, and I empty myself of all desire and want and regret. As the men below defile my body to ensure I'll never rise again, I surrender to the pull of the dappled gray stag who prances toward me. If I leap onto his back, he will carry me to the Otherworld. The land of light and bottomless cauldrons will offer me rest until it is my time to live again. Until it is my time to seek retribution for all the wrongs I have suffered this day.

Chapter Twenty-Four

Galanta

I become one of the creatures I once feared. I scour fields of carnage in the name of my mistress with a hooked beak and wings of violet streaked night.

I come to love the slice of wind through my feathers. I abandon the cage of mortal weakness and time is a shadow that passes with no meaning.

When I woke from my slumber, I was forever altered. The cleaving from everyone and everything I once knew was the beginning.

In exchange for my life, the Goddess demanded my servitude. Two of her crow maidens helped me recover his body from the pit of earth they threw him into. They helped me swath him in seaweed to hold him together and swam with me to the bottom of the cove where I laid him to rest.

The goddess told me he would not lie there forever. That one day, she would let me leave her side to rouse him from his slumber. She told me his immortal soul still lingers and it is full of rage and sorrow. She said that even though he resides in the Otherworld and should have no cares, he holds onto his need for vengeance. She said he is not ready to abandon it and accept the mantle of his responsibility.

And she told me I am not ready to give him the patience and fortitude he needs.

So I will do her bidding and reap the souls of those fallen in battle. I will become nothing more than one of her couriers, and let the wind sough through my wings.

Until she decides I have served her long enough.

Part II

"Your indenture is at end. It is time for you to resurrect your mate."

After thousands of battles, I never thought to hear those words. I open my mouth, and nothing emerges but a hoarse caw. The weapons of war have morphed into monsters I could not have imagined. Far more dangerous and destructive than my mate's hooves and teeth. I dove through cannon fire, and flew high as winged machines circled each other in an aerial ballet. The ravages of war have soaked into my very soul.

"Though I have given you near immortality, you will need to find your humanity again. You must find the answers in the each uisge court."

She snaps her fingers in the air and when the sparks settle, a long cloak of feathers covers my pale limbs. It swathes me from head to toe.

"Much has changed. In the world and in the court. Your mate's twin has found his mate and prepares to ascend the throne. You must convince them to give you access to the library. The lore you need to restore the balance we lost is there."

"They will not welcome me." The words are no more than a croak and my human tongue feels like a boulder.

"No. They will not. You must convince them nonetheless."

"What if I cannot?"

"Failure is an unacceptable outcome. Everything depends on your success."

"Success should not hinge on the strength of my persuasiveness."

"Show some gratitude, girl. Though you haven't spoken of it, I've felt your pining. You've not forgotten him, and you want nothing more than to make amends. This is your chance. Take it."

I'm afraid to take it. She said the world has changed. How much has it changed? How many years have passed since I let the breeze ruffle my feathers for the first time?

"You will recognize the islands. But not the dwellings. Or the inhabitants. Or anything else. We are all in grave danger and the wheel of time cannot begin its next rotation until you fulfill your duty."

Chapter Twenty-Five

Galanta

For over a thousand years I have witnessed the rise and fall of mortal kingdoms. For over a thousand years I have carried the astonished, the angry and the resigned to their final berths. I have walked the battlefield and haunted the black air. Because I have seen so much sorrow and rage, I do not blame Eachann's brother for his anger. Witnessing all the atrocities and waste taught me the grace and fortitude the Goddess ensured me I would need for the task ahead. The warlord is now the heir apparent and he has no reason to accept my profession of innocence when his brother perished for my sake. When my lover slaughtered the priest and the witch hunter, he sealed his fate. He wreaked vengeance on my behalf and my village exacted retribution in the name of the church.

His warlord brother hasn't forgiven me.

My mistress offered no advice on how to approach my mate's court. So I have thrown myself upon its mercy.

It is clear that Eachann's aunt and uncle are using me to goad their nephew. And that any mercy they extend is a ploy. But I will accept it because I have no other choice. I need access to the library if I am ever going to bring him back.

Callum spares me a brief, furious glance. "What is she doing here?"

"I am here to set things right. I've been trying to make amends for over a thousand years. Whether you believe me or not, I'll continue to do so."

His gaze rakes me up and down. "I'd love to hear about your efforts, Galanta. From where I'm standing it looks like nothing has changed."

"I made sure my family suffered." As one of Morrigan's ravens I haunted their dreams with blood and death. They all died alone and quavering and forgotten. "They told me the man I loved was an abomination. When they slayed your brother in the cove, it wasn't at my behest."

"What proof do you offer?" He scoffs.

Queen Creiddylad is watching our riposte with a pleased smile. Like a cat that has just swallowed a mouse.

"I don't expect you to take my claims at face value. I thought it was important I confront you face to face and tell you I had absolutely nothing to do with his death."

"You were the one that made the assignation. And you lured him to his death after he saved you from burning."

"I was losing the babe in my womb as your brother was losing his life. My family and the church wanted every trace of him obliterated."

The woman beside Callum places her hand on his arm, as if she'd holding him back. "That's terrible." Her expression is full of pity.

"Your heart is too tender, wife."

So she is Callum's mate. Eachann proclaimed it would likely never happen. Because of Callum's disdain for mortals and his refusal to engage his emotions.

Unlike his wife, my plight does not move him to pity. His expression is grim. "Whether or not you wielded the sword, you are indirectly responsible for his death. The blame lies solely on your shoulders. They attacked him because he sought retribution for their treatment of you."

"No one bears the wounds of that truth as heavily as me."

"You are unwelcome here."

I close my eyes at the truth of his words. I held the faint hope that I could explain what happened, and somehow be reconciled with his family. "I know I am unwelcome. I only wish to study the scrolls housed in the clan library. I want to find a way to bring him back."

"You may as well lasso the moon. It's impossible. You must accept the consequences of your actions."

I raise my hands in supplication. "Please."

He visibly recoils.

"Please." I don't know if the tale of my ordeal will be believed, so I alter it to make it more digestible. "I had a dream the night of his death. I wrapped his corpse in the shroud of the bloodied sheets and walked beyond where the sea meets the sunrise. I covered the shroud in kelp and placed him beneath the waves. My dreams told me he would be restored in a thousand years if I could find the appropriate incantation in the annals of your kind."

"Why would the gods deign to visit an unmated human?"

"I may not bear your brother's sigil, but we were mated. And my line are descended from the goddess Morrigan herself and have served her for millennia."

"Nephew, who knows why the gods have chosen to meddle. It is not for us to question it; I see no harm in letting the girl indulge her fancy or allowing her this boon."

"She's not entitled to a boon," Callum snarls.

An elderly each uisge woman with a cane steps forward. "I agree with Prince Callum."

This is a play for power and I don't know why the queen has chosen to use me.

Callum and his mate step away, and it appears from their earnest conversation that she may be arguing on my behalf. I pray to the goddess it is so.

When they approach again, Callum's expression is one of resignation.

He turns to his aunt and uncle. "Fine. She has six weeks to find what she's looking for. If she hasn't found it by that time, she'll face a tribune of brehons to determine her fate."

I want to sink to the floor in relief. But I clench my fists and bow my head. The queen nods almost imperceptibly to one of her handmaidens and she gestures for me to follow.

The court is in a furor. Sabhinion is back. She disappeared after the coup and has been absent ever since. I know she is a scholar and I hope she will assist me. I've spent three weeks searching for answers to no avail because many of the manuscripts are in tongues I cannot read.

When I finally gather the courage to approach her, she is loitering in the corner of the dining hall with Callum and his wife. I am glad to see Sabhinion again. Her gaze is not hostile like that of her brother, merely curious. And I sense sympathy from Callum's human mate.

He is annoyed by my interruption. "My aunt and uncle may welcome you to this court because I have yet to ascend the throne, but mark me, witch, I will not be as forgiving or tolerant. If you have not found the answers you seek when the sands in the hourglass expire, you'll submit yourself to trial for your treason."

Callum's mate looks irritated at his pronouncement. She steps forward and catches my hands in hers. "I will have words again with my husband. He can be harsh at times. I am a scholar by training, what is known as a research librarian, and I want to help you find the answers you seek. Everyone seems to believe the prophecy is inescapable and I'd like to prove them wrong."

"There is a prophecy?"

"Yes. We found it after Eachann was killed. I will show it to you." Sabhinion answers. She walks away and I trail in her wake, because the imperious wave of her hand apparently means I should follow her now.

I scurry behind until I catch up to her athletic stride. She's tall, even for her kind. As tall as her brothers. Carrig is the only each uisge I've seen who is taller than her.

"You do not blame me for his death."

She shrugs and whirls to face me. "No, Galanta, I do not blame you. My brother's passionate defense of you led to his death. Whether you remember it or not, you tried to persuade him against revenge. I was there and know he paid you no heed. As soon as he left your bedside he sharpened his swords."

When she swings open the heavy wooden doors to the library, I gingerly step inside. The ceiling rises so far above me, I can barely make out the skylight. There are books everywhere. The shelves begin at floor-level and go up and up and up. Sabh chuckles when she notices I've stopped.

"It can be quite daunting. You should let me give you a full tour once I show you the scroll."

She makes her way to the middle of the cavernous room. There's a huge drafting table that holds a scroll flattened and anchored on all four corners.

"Though I can read runes, I only know a smattering of Greek and Latin."

"This is in Old Elvish, so I'll translate it for you. And I can loan you some of my lexicons so the learning goes faster. This is one of the few documents that hasn't been translated into one of the classical languages."

She runs a reverent hand over the parchment to smooth out the wrinkles. "The wind on the water is stronger than the oak of the mightiest fleet, Than all the warriors standing tall. It is here sorrow and chaos will meet, And the kingdom of kelp and brine shall fall. The prince shall reclaim his throne, and save what she sought to destroy. The sacrifice will be heart and bone, And love the binding alloy."

"You've figured out what it means and who it's about?"

"Yes. It's obviously about Callum and Meghan."

"It could just as easily be about Eachann and I."

"Eachann is dead. I know you want to bring him back because you think some sort of atonement is required of you, but I don't think it's possible. All empirical evidence would point to the contrary."

"You mean the wealth of information we have about the Otherworld and what happens there?" I sarcastically point out. Because we don't have a wealth of information. We barely have any information. That's why I'm here. It's my last resort.

She eyes me shrewdly. "You're right. We don't have very much information. Which means that once people go there, they never want to leave. What makes you think my brother would be any different?"

"Morrigan assured me that he was. She said he hasn't forgotten his need for revenge or accepted his fate. She said he is only biding his time until he is resurrected."

"Isn't that a resurrection as a new creature though? I've never heard of anyone being resurrected to resolve unfinished business."

"The Goddess was adamant. When I served as one of her couriers, she sent me far and wide. And you're right. I've never heard of someone being resurrected back into themselves. But that is what she claims it is my mission to do."

"I will do all I can to help you. I've catalogued most of the library. My aunt and uncle weren't known for their scholarly pursuits, and they added very little to the collection during their reign. Callum has given me leave to correct that, though, and to digitize all the files we have."

"That will take hundreds of years," I observe as I look around.

She shrugs and gives me an insouciant grin. "Which I just happen to have at my disposal. Now, what I don't have is a thorough understanding of the duties and obligations of the servants of Morrigan. Did she transform you or did you perform your duties as you are now?"

"She transformed me. I served as one of her ravens for what I now know was well over a thousand years. Through all the great wars. I have learned that the more things change, the more they stay the same. And that humankind can be even more incredibly selfish and greedy than I first believed."

Sabhinion looks fascinated. "Will you write it all down for me when you can find the time?"

"Of course."

She claps her hands together. "It will be quite the addition to our library!"

"I'll start on it after I finish my research. Speaking of which, where should I begin?"

"I've already had one of the administrators begin pulling sources you may find useful. That's the first stack over there."

She points to a pile so high it looks ready to topple over. "I'll get started then. Thank you for sharing the prophecy with me."

Chapter Twenty-Six

Galanta

"You should read these." Meghan tells me, and gestures toward the books she's been shelving. Callum promised her she could have the romance bookstore she's always dreamt of, and the first shipment of stock just came in. She chose as cozy cottage on the outskirts of the village, and we've spent the last two weeks painting the walls and picking out comfortable chairs. There's a huge bay window that looks out on the ocean, and even on a quiet day you can hear the pounding of the waves far below.

"Why should I read them?"

"You should read them because they're all about fated mates." Sabh explains.

"Do they end in tragedy?" Until I bring him back, and I'm confident I will, even on the days all I feel is despair, reading about happy endings and seeing the easy, peaceful, supportive love Callum and Meghan share fills me with both longing and envy. I don't know if I have the fortitude to read those kinds of stories yet.

"The couples all have unique journeys, but none of them end in tragedy." Meghan sets Mabh in her playpen and lays a hand on my shoulder. "But I understand if it sounds like something hard to absorb right now."

Sabh shoots her a look and I'm sure they're sharing a loaded glance over my head.

She clears her throat. "Galanta, have you thought about what will happen, or what you'll do, if you can't bring him back?"

I haven't let myself think about it. Because if I can't bring him back I don't know what all of it was for. "I'm not giving up hope."

"We're not saying it's hopeless, we just think you need to be realistic. We all know the gods are fickle and cryptic and maybe this wasn't what they meant at all and you're just a way for them to amuse themselves. You should prepare yourself for disappointment."

I know she's trying to help me, but I can't hold back my resentment. She can say I should prepare myself - she has the man she loves in her arms every night and two children they both dote on. I've made so many sacrifices. I won't sacrifice this. "Are the two of you saying you grow weary of helping me? Of looking for a needle in a haystack?"

The library holds nothing of value to my mission. I have sought out the remotest parts of it and all my efforts have been futile. If there is a reversal spell somewhere in this library, it is determined to remain hidden.

The timeline Callum gave me came and went. He hasn't banished me, and I suspect his reluctance to cast me out is due to his fear of retaliation from his mate. Meghan miraculously survived the sacrificial ceremony, and she has taken me under her wing. The goddess Cliodhna intervened, and she recently gave birth to her second child. A girl they named Mabh.

I know she believes the prophecy is about me. That if I succeed in raising my mate, I will meet my death. I think it's why she'll tolerate no aspersions being cast in my direction. Sabh is an ally as well. They told me it's because they've both been plagued by male idiocy and share my frustration at the lack of progress we're making in our research. The men were completely unhelpful until Sabh very insistently demanded Carrig lend his expertise with ancient languages. He grumbled at first, but his translation of some of the oldest sources has proven invaluable.

We are on the verge of discovery – I feel it just beyond our grasp.

"I found something," Meghan calls out. I want to peer over her shoulder, but her warlord husband, who still blames me for his brother's death, looms out of the shadows. I slip away because I am too exhausted to face his hostile glare. Later, I'll ask his wife to share whatever she found.

The fairy tale I found months ago is the only promising clue we have. And it is only a fanciful retelling of the day Eachann and I met.

To ensure I don't encounter anyone who will sap away what little energy I have with their misdirected ill will, I take the long route back to my chamber. I'm walking through the oldest part of the castle everyone claims is haunted when I hear the first whisper.

"You need the diary."

I whip my head about because I thought I was alone. It sounded like they were standing right beside me. "Who's there? Show yourself."

I'm not afraid of ghosts. Especially not the ones here. They seem benign except for their tendency to gossip. They don't seem the least bit malicious, and even if they were, the crystal draped around my neck protects me.

"There's nothing to show. If you want to right the wrongs you believe you've caused, find the diary."

"What diary? Is it in the library?"

"All the diaries of the queens are housed there. Queen's Badb's as well. When our kingdom began she inscribed all the sands of time and songs of making in her diary."

"So hers is the diary I'm searching for? And I need a song of making?"

Sunlight suddenly pours through the stained-glass window high in the wall. When the dust motes settle, I use my hand to shade my eyes. The scene portrayed is one of Queen Badb. She's standing on a cliff overlooking the sea, holding a rowan branch. It's the same tapestry that hangs in the throne room.

"A song of making will call the Golden Prince back from the Otherworld."

Songs of making are the oldest magic. They are what binds the world together. "I am not powerful enough to wield a song of making."

"Morrigan obviously didn't choose you for your looks. Use your gifts, girl. That's what they're for."

I know I'm not a great beauty like Helen of Troy. My scars and my pain are too visible for that. But at least I'm not a literal bag of bones stuck in a crypt somewhere.

"We heard that."

"My apologies. I didn't realize I'd spoken aloud."

There's an audible sniff. "Hmmph. We shall take no offense this time. However, see that you temper your future approach with the respect due our station and wisdom."

"Of course." Since I have no idea which of the ancient court has deemed to help me, it's basically a platitude. But it seems to pacify them because there's a hum of assent.

"I humbly thank you for your assistance."

"We grew weary of seeing the lot of you bumble about like idiots. Your efforts gave us the megrims, which we thought ourselves impervious to. Trust me, it was our pleasure to help in whatever way we could."

"May I have a name since I do not have a face to express my gratitude toward?"

"I am known as Einoringen. I was once the chief bard and scholar. Sabhinion and Carrig spent many years under my tutelage and it pains me to see them so incompetent."

So he was a harsh taskmaster. "No offense, Master Einoringen. I don't believe it's incompetence. Sabh has thoroughly catalogued and reorganized the library. It's that there is a lack of pertinent material on the subject."

He harrumphs dismissively again. "I see those two have already forgotten the first research lesson I taught them. Always examine the primary source documents first. The search should have begun with a meticulous examination of all the diary and journal collection. Once all such sources have been eliminated from consideration, a well-trained scholar focuses on others."

Sabh and Carrig have been leading our expedition, but they're as caught up in their constant game of bickering and one-upmanship as they are in our mission. They're always trying to best each other. It's exhausting to watch. I guess they find each other so distracting they've forgotten the lessons this ghost drilled into their heads once upon a time.

"I'll be sure to remind them of their training," I reassure my incorporeal advisor.

"Not that it will have any effect."

I curtsey in the general direction of the disembodied voice. "I shall remind them all the same. I bid you good evening, Sir Einoringen."

The diary was hidden in the library's darkest corner. Stacked in the middle of a pile on a shelf full of ledgers about hatchery yields and tithes. Where the smell of old leather and musty paper fills your nostrils. When I finally found it, I kept the discovery to myself. Meghan and Callum were still recovering from the shock of her almost sacrifice, and Carrig and Sabh were researching something for her great-aunt. Since the coronation of the royal couple and the birth of their daughter, no one but me seems to believe there's a way to bring him back. They indulge me with polite inquiries, but I can tell their minds are elsewhere.

The ghosts spoke the truth. The first each uisge queen was wise in lore and magic. One of her diary entries held the spell I needed to bring him back to me. The words

were in the old tongue, but the lexicon Sabh
gave me helped me puzzle through the unfamiliar
pronunciation. I've memorized the incantation, and I
hope it is enough to restore my prince.

If I tell his brother and sister about my find, and
the spell doesn't work, it will just make things worse.
Especially with the king, who still barely tolerates me
despite my friendship with his wife.

So I rowed myself to the circle of stones at Soay.
According to Badb's diary, this is an ancient seat of
power and will magnify my own.

Meghan told me that crossing your fingers brings
good luck, and I'm tempted to do it before I raise my
arms in the direction of the setting sun.

I close my eyes and the power sends tingles down my
spine before it lights me up from within. My hands
glow a faint green, and my veins writhe like vines
beneath my skin. The crystal is blazing hot beneath my
kirtle, and its white light twists around the ribbons of
green swirling through the stones.

There is a clap of thunder and one of the menhirs
cracks down the middle.

A whirlpool forms in the cove below and I watch as
something large and dark emerges from its center.

It can only be him. But the shadow rising from the water is taller and broader than I remember. His strides churn the waves around him as he marches toward me. He's glowering, and his fists are clenched at his sides. He is altered. I can see it from here.

He is full of thunder and anger. When his gaze lands on me, I know I am the source of whatever boils beneath the surface and will be the one who surrenders to it. Because my love once rendered him the victim of a brutal plot. I don't know what he felt in that moment he thought I'd betrayed him. I don't know if he was overwhelmed by sorrow or fury, or what forged him into this creature I don't recognize.

He steps ashore and halts mere inches from me. I swallow my fear and clench my own fists. I have suffered this agony for over a thousand years, searching for a way to give us more than the tragedy we became. Now he stands before me and I know that he's still my golden prince, full of laughter and passion beneath his resentment.

"You."

There is the sweep of arctic wind in his voice.

"Me."

"All of it was because of you and your treachery."

"There was no treachery."

"Lies," he scoffs.

"Not lies. Everything I did was for love of you and our babe."

"And where is our babe now?"

"I lost him."

"You killed him with your scheming and your poisons. I know it was all a trap, witch. And I'll never forgive you."

I take a deep breath and push down the jagged pain caused by his words. "I am not your enemy."

His laughter isn't the cascade of sunlight I remember. It's brittle and harsh. Like the crack and fall of branches weighted by snow. "If you are not my enemy, I have none. Your false heart and vicious plotting ended the life I knew."

"My heart was never false. The manipulative scheming of your aunt and uncle made your kingdom rot from the inside out."

"They will feel my wrath first. I have other plans for you."

"Your brother Callum already ensured they were brought to trial for treason. The brehon sentenced them to death at the hands of the wild Kraken. They are naught but bones buried fathoms deep."

I know I will toss and turn all night considering the plans he has for me.

"Callum is alive?" His expression is relieved.

"He is. I will take you to him." I turn away so my gaze won't linger on the carved beauty of his naked form.

Chapter Twenty-Seven

Eachann

“There is something you should know.”

She interrupts my spiraling thoughts.

"Something besides the fact your kin murdered me and somehow your infernal magic resurrected me over a thousand years later?"

"Yes. There is more."

I come to a halt and whirl to face her. We are at the edge of the long sea wall, and I cross my arms and lean against it.

"Spill your truths, witch."

"There is a prophecy. That is why Sabhinion decreed we must marry."

"Thousands of years could pass and my sister would still not have changed. I see she is still adroitly maneuvering our lives to suit her purposes."

"I was a servant of Morrigan. She whisked me away to her hall when I would have taken my own life. My indenture ended and she sent me back here with all the knowledge I've gleaned for your sake."

Knowing she has not long been in this new world either somehow makes it more bearable.

"Morrigan? She has no servants, only ravens."

"Yes. As was I. While you lay buried beneath the waves, I was witness to countless wars. When soldiers fell, I led their souls to rest. I had wings."

She sounds wistful.

"You were incorporeal?"

"No. I became one of her ravens. That is how she chooses us. Her couriers are not only warriors felled in battle. They are also the witches who have loyally served her."

"And Morrigan banished you from her side as I wish to do?"

"She did not banish me. She told me there is a season and a time for every trial and triumph and my time of trial was nearly at an end."

"And now you seek to triumph? What you have done is not a triumph, witch."

"I brought you back. Knowing that you are once again standing in front of me, breathing, is a triumph. Even though you are bristling with anger and bitterness, I will claim this victory."

"You brought me back to what? This world is nothing like the one I left. My kingdom is on the brink of collapse from insurrection and corruption. Callum should be ruling in my stead."

"He should not. Because the prophecy is not about your brother and his mate. It is about us. I once knew joy at your hands, and though I will never know it again, it was enough."

"Enough for what, witch? Enough for you to slip beneath my defenses?"

"No. Enough to sustain me when we do what we must."

"What does the prophecy say we must do?"

"I must die at your hands. A sacrifice."

I plotted revenge while I was trapped in my watery tomb. I imagined all the ways I would strangle her with seaweed and plunge my dagger into her breast. I imagined drawing and quartering her, of starving her to death. All those dark desires are hollow and I am a fool. Because the sound of her voice and the hook of her smile reel me in now just as they did then.

I am not vindicated by her revelation. Her death will satisfy far more than my need for revenge, but I question my fortitude. My beast roars inside at her presence, his hooves swift and furious. His impatience and desire to claim echo through the changeling half of my soul and I know it will be nigh impossible to deny him. Killing her will prove the hardest thing I have ever done because it will go against my very nature.

"When is this sacrifice to take place?"

"Your sister claims your succession must be secure or it is all for naught. Though Callum and Meghan have ruled in your stead, your return means they must abdicate and allow you to ascend to your rightful place. The kingdom clamors for stability and I must bear your son."

"You are telling me I must bend you, the woman I despise more than any other creature, to my bidding."

She shrugs, but it's anything but a gesture of nonchalance. Her expression is too stark and her grip in the folds of her dress is white knuckled. "Yes. The manner of the bedding makes no difference."

"And once you bear our son? What then, witch?"

"Once he is grown enough to wean from my breast, my time runs out. You will sink your dagger into me and watch my blood mix with the sea as I drown beneath the waves."

"Where has your wildness gone? You would so readily accept death at my hand?"

"I have lived a long life, though not all of it as mortal or even human. But it is more than I ever expected when you rescued me from the flames. Of course I want more. But the one person I would give my eternity to cannot bear the sight of me."

I harden my resolve against her. "Surely you are not asking me to forget how we came to be here?"

Her bark of laughter is the crash of the sea upon the rocks. "You have made it patently obvious you will never again show mercy toward me or my kind. Be they mortal or witch, you will not waver. You would rather dwell in your anger than the moments of joy and hope we once shared."

"My brother was fond of telling me I was too trusting, and gave my heart to those who were unworthy of it. He rescued me more than once from my folly and I never lost the hope that one day my instincts would prove right. And then I met you."

"And then you met me."

"And I gave my heart to you more wholly than I had ever given it. And it may as well have been your hand that carved it from my chest."

"I know you will never believe me, but I did not betray you. I don't know how my family discovered you were meeting me or where you were coming ashore. I wanted to escape with you."

I clench my fists against the urge to press her into the wall at her back. My hands around her neck, throttling her as she sinks against the plaster. "Then where were you? Did you watch from the safety of the harbor as they cut us down like swine?"

"I was still in the grove. I went there to retrieve my family's legacy as we agreed. I lost our babe there to the poison of our enemies."

"A likely excuse."

"I would not lie. I wanted our babe."

"I thought you wanted our babe. But your betrayal tells me otherwise."

"If I could have been there, I would have been. If I knew what they planned, I would have warned you."

"If you were poisoned, how did you survive?"

"I didn't. I lost the babe in a torrent of blood that killed me. Or nearly killed me. I hovered on the brink of life and death and stretched my hand out to clasp that of Annwn and his reapers. The Morrigan hauled me from his clutches."

"Why would the goddess show you such favor?"

"She wanted my servitude. And she claimed I was meant for more than dying in such a way. She told me you were gone – that you'd been slaughtered. There was nothing more for me to cling to or believe in. But she would not let my self-pity stand."

"The prophecy is in her tongue?"

"No, according to your sister, a selkie seeress made it known. The entire kingdom was taught to recite it, and knows it by heart. Your uncle's greed caused nothing but millennia of hardship and suffering, and they needed something to place their hope in."

"What catastrophe will befall us if the prophecy is thwarted?"

"Sabhinion believes the each uisge will fade behind the veil, just as the Tuatha de Danaan did, if the prophecy isn't fulfilled."

Though it left my rage undiminished, my time in the Otherworld has given me perspective. "All things must end in their own time. That is the purpose of the Great Wheel upon which we all turn."

"None of us want to believe this is the end of the each uisge. Especially Callum and Meghan. They revel in the rise of a new generation, and the birth of their daughter has been hailed as an end to the harrowing events of the past."

"I will gladly kill you, witch. For more reasons than I can name. But even that act may not ward us against the cataclysm to come."

"We must try. We must exchange the sigils and see what comes."

She drops into an abbreviated curtsey and turns on her heel. I follow in her wake, eager for the reunion with my siblings.

When his gaze lands on me, my brother's face splits into the widest grin I have ever seen. He barrels toward me, and his hug is fierce. His cheek is wet against mine.

"I prayed this day would come."

My brother has changed. There is a light and peace in him. When he looks down at the dark-haired woman who sidles up to him, I know why. His contentment comes from her. She carries a babe in her arms who coos and raises its arms.

Callum scoops up the babe and slips his arm around the woman's waist. When he turns to me again, there are tears of joy in his eyes.

"Brother, meet my mate, Meghan, and our daughter, Mabh."

I feel the sting of my own tears behind my eyes. "Our family has grown."

Meghan steps forward and rises to her toes. The peck on my cheek startles me. "I have heard much of you, Eachann Lir."

"Brother!" Sabhinion hurtles into me, sobbing. "She did it. She truly did it. She brought you back to us." She clasps my face in her palms and touches her forehead to mine. "I have missed you more than you'll ever know, you dunderhead."

Carrig is next. His hug is brief, and the clap on my back nearly fells me. His breadth is even more foreboding than it was then, but his eyes glint with unshed tears. Just like those of everyone else.

Galanta stands on the edge of our gathering, but steps forward when Callum beckons her with a crooked finger. "I may yet learn to forgive you, green witch." He dips his head in acknowledgment. "You have my gratitude."

She dips her head in return, but her gaze remains wary. "I only seek to right the wrongs that were done."

"Come brother. We will feast and regale each other with our tales."

He hands the babe back to Meghan and throws his arm over my shoulder.

When I look back, the woman who shattered my soul meets my gaze with an unflinching one of her own.

My belly full, I push away from the table. Carrig and Callum are sprawled on the bench across from me, their hands crossed over their stomachs. They look positively beatific.

"I invited Duncan here because I only understand half of what he says. He needs to tell you what's happening to the islands."

I straighten in alarm. "What is happening to the islands?"

"The sea is destroying them. I don't understand all the science of it. Duncan can explain it far better. But you need to know what's at stake – why everyone believes the prophecy's so damned important."

As if we've summoned him, I hear my cousin's hearty laugh. Callum shakes his head. "That would be my mate. They are thick as thieves – usually at my expense."

When he strides into the room and sees me, the bundle of papers he has under his arm scatter across the floor. "If I didn't believe my own eyes..." He murmurs.

His hug is like that of one of the bears that fishes on the ice. He's not as tall as the rest of us, but his shoulders are twice as broad.

"I missed ye, cousin. We have need of your music."

It's the first time anyone's mentioned my music. The melody that filled my heart when I first found my mate is muted now. "I don't know if music is still a part of me."

His heavy hand squeezes my shoulder. "Ye'll find it again. You loved it as much as I love the science of how things work."

"Mayhap ye could come up with a lullaby? Wee Mabh is a fitful sleeper and keeps Meghan and I from our own rest."

Callum's suggestion may be the motivation I need and will give me something to occupy my days besides thoughts of her and the perpetual gloom that hangs over all our heads. Our grandmother was one of the sirens and taught me everything she knew before she died. Helping my wee niece sleep is a fitting way to reawaken my gift.

Duncan unrolls a piece of parchment on the table and anchors its corners with our steins. "You'll need something stronger than ale for what I'm about to share."

Carrig rubs his hands together. "I have just the thing."

Once he disappears, Callum turns to me. "One of the things he's managed to perfect in our absence is spirits. He ferments the wheat and sugar and whatever else he adds to it in an oak barrel for years. You'll enjoy it. And it'll make Duncan's news easier to digest."

Duncan has been talking for at least an hour and we're on our third bottle. I have many questions. Most of them lead to even more questions. But there's one that burns above all the others. "Do you believe this prophecy is the answer?"

He removes his spectacles and rubs his fingers over the crease between his brows. "No."

"But ---" Callum interjects. Duncan cuts him off with an abrupt wave of his hand.

"Why don't you think it's the answer?"

"Because magic is never the answer. I am a man of science and I trust what the data is telling me. Magic isn't going to reverse what's happening to the islands. It was caused by humankind and they're the only ones who can fix it."

Carrig audibly scoffs. "No offense, mate, but they don't seem eager to fix what they broke."

"I don't understand how things could have changed so much. We lived the same way for thousands of years, and then it all goes ass up in less than three hundred?"

Callum snorts and points at Duncan. "You can blame it on his science."

"It's not my science. It's the throw-away economy. The consumerism and the capitalism and the bigger and better and more is always better mentality."

They're glaring at each other, and I can tell this is not their first debate on the subject.

"Protecting this kingdom is my responsibility now. I need solutions, not complaints."

"I always knew you were a peacemaker at heart." Carrig winks. "It's that golden sunlight on yer hair, cailin ban."

I groan at the nickname but am glad his teasing lightened the mood and diffused the tension.

"I thought I'd find you here." Callum closes the door to the music room and leans against it.

The world has greatly changed. Callum assured me I'll become accustomed to all the modern trappings, but with every discovery I make of this new world I feel more like a fish, flopping and stranded on the beach.

"I've been sitting here for hours. Just staring at it. When I run my fingers over the strings, there's no melody. All I hear is a bunch of jumbled notes that don't make any sense and defy arrangement."

"I think your mind's on other things and its blocking the inspiration."

I frown. "You think I should forgive her."

"I'm not as convinced of her innocence as my wife, but I think she at least deserves your compassion."

"My compassion? For what? She's the instrument of her own destruction. Everything that happened to us was her fault."

"I think you want to forgive her. I think you know she isn't the one to blame. But you've held onto your anger for so long, you don't know how to move past it."

"Is that why you think I can't make sense of the music?"

"Yes. But I don't think you'll ever admit it to yourself."

He steps further into the room and settles in the chair directly across from me. "Do you know what I remember about the summer our father handed us our first swords?"

I grunt in response. "I'm sure you're going to tell me. Whether or not I want to hear it."

"You're such a prig, sometimes. I remember how excited I was. How I tossed that wooden blade around and capered like it was the best day of my life. You did exactly the opposite. You turned it over and over in your hands and your eyes strayed to the harp you'd propped up in the corner of the room. You couldn't tear your gaze away from it. You never wanted to hold a sword."

"I do what I must. As I've always done."

"But you don't need to hold a sword unless it's to protect the people you love. I'm here to bear the sword. Find your music again, brother. I miss it."

"I miss it too," I hoarsely confess. "But I don't know where I left it."

"I do. That morning in the weapons room, you taught us some bawdy song you heard the soldiers singing. It was the last time I heard you sing. We need your music to remind us why we're holding the swords."

He closes the door quietly behind him and I sit in the dark and ponder his words. Was that truly the day I left my music behind?

Was it just because Father handed me a sword? Or was it because Grandmother was gone? She'd set out in her skiff a fortnight earlier with a single flask of water and a piece of gold to ease her journey to the Otherworld. I was still raw with her absence, but I let the harp hold my sorrow when it became too much to keep inside me.

Chapter Twenty-Eight

Galanta

I knew his welcome would be joyful. I don't regret keeping the spell to myself. I didn't want to give them false hope if my efforts failed as they have done in the past.

Now I know he blames me for all of it and there is nothing I can do to convince him of my innocence. I was a fool to believe everything would be as it was before. That he would wrap me in his arms and call me his wild heart. I fear I will never again hear those words. I fear that when he comes to my bed it will be with a heart and touch full of ice. With no mercy and no tenderness. With no remnant of what we once were to each other or any memory of the pledges we made.

"You must give him time." Meghan's soft words interrupt my brooding.

"He thinks I betrayed him. That I used him. He will never forgive me. I'll die looking into eyes full of nothing but hatred."

"You know how obstinate he can be. It is in their nature to be contrary. You must persevere."

"I will do what I must. I have told him of the prophecy."

She laughs darkly. "That infernal prophecy. I wish we could find a means of deflating its power. It has this whole kingdom in a chokehold."

"Will we continue to search for a way to overturn it?"

"We must. After all we've been through, we deserve our happily ever after."

"He seemed eager at the prospect of slitting my throat." My tone is laced with the bitterness of our exchange.

"You must be patient. He will need you. He will need all of us. And be prepared for Arianrhod to take you under her wing. She'll insist you learn the sigils you need for the ceremony inside out."

I'm nose deep in a Norse folktale, looking for clues to the reversal of the prophecy, when Arianrhod finds me.

"I know you thought to escape me, girl. I hate to disappoint you, but you have much to learn in a week's time. We can wait no longer than that for your mate to claim his crown."

"Meghan told me I must learn sigils."

She must hear the thread of alarm in my voice, because she snorts. "Only two, chit. Don't lose your breakfast."

"Why only two?"

"Because you will only carve two of them."

"Where am I going to carve them?"

"You'll carve them on your mate's skin. You must bind his beast and tether his soul to the here and now."

"So they are not common sigils?"

"Those of the binding are no longer taught – merely passed down from generation to generation."

Once we're in her study, she hands me paper and charcoal and sets me to work. Hours pass, and I don't even realize she left me to my solitude until I see the flicker of the setting sun through the window. I've likely missed the evening meal, so I'll have to make do with whatever I can scrounge from the kitchens. Thank goodness Meghan's pregnancy cravings mean the pantry is well stocked with what she calls junk food.

I steal one of the buttery movie microwave popcorn bags from her stash and grab a soda from the fridge. I'm making my way to the dining hall when I hear his laughter.

I have to brace myself against the wall. He hasn't laughed anywhere near me since his return. I missed the rumbling warmth of it – the way it felt when I laid my ear against his chest. I can't be near it right now. I'll start weeping. I don't want him to see my weakness and he'll probably scoff at me.

I retreat to the familiarity of the library. There are so many sections we haven't explored yet – surely one of them holds the answers we seek.

There's a promising title on the top shelf. It has gilt lettering down the spine I now recognize as Old Elvish, and the leather binding is cracked and worn with age. I manage to wrap my fingers around it and nearly have it extracted when I lose my footing. I try to wrap my leg around the side of the ladder as it teeters precariously. The book is heavy, and I have to use both arms to hold it.

I'm falling backward and scrambling for purchase when a hard hand lands in the middle of my back. The pressure pins me to the rungs and halts my tumble.

The book is lifted from my arms and I hear the thump of it landing on the table behind me. "You snuck away, witch."

My body tenses beneath his heated palm. It rests at the base of my spine, and his long fingers curve over the rise of my body.

"I didn't want to waste time. And I knew you would not miss me." I want to swallow the confession as soon as it leaves my lips.

"I missed you, witch." His palm glides lower and he pinches me. When I inhale, the other palm lands against me with a resounding smack. "You deserve my hands on you like this. But my own body betrays me."

I whimper when he presses closer, the long ridge of him burning through every single layer of our clothing. He buries his face in my hair and nips my ear. I'm incapable of speech right now.

"My cock remembers how you feel and wants to fill you. But my heart wants to defile you and punish you for your betrayal."

I grip the ladder so I won't reach backward and grip his length instead.

He twists me around and works his hand beneath the waistband of my jeans. One blunt finger strokes me through the lacy underwear, and he leans forward. He bites my collarbone and slips his hand under the elastic. I rise to my toes when he thrusts two fingers into me. I'm soaking wet. I've been wet since he strode from the waves, his naked body gleaming with salt and runes.

"So fucking tight for me," he groans and plunges into me again. I gasp when his knuckles scrape against my walls.

"I want to see your wet pussy fuck my fingers, witch." He withdraws his fingers and unfastens my pants. He yanks the denim to my ankles but leaves the lace intact.

He pulls it tight, until it's a thread of fabric that splays me wide open. His eyes glitter as he cups me, and I bite my lip to keep from screaming in frustration. His knuckle strokes me over the fabric.

"Stop tormenting me," I croak.

He drops to a crouch so the lace is even with his mouth. His hot breath turns me into a puddle of molten lava and when he strokes me with the flat of his tongue it feels like my veins are going to burst through my skin.

I don't want the lace between us. I want him to rip it off.

"Get rid of it."

"No." He brushes across me again and rises to his feet. "I'm going to make you look presentable. So no one will know you're wet and you just begged me to touch you. But I'm not adjusting these." He snaps the elastic at my waist. "I want you to soak this fucking lace every time you take a step and think about how much better my tongue would feel."

"Why are you denying me? Why are you denying yourself? I can feel how much you want it too." I cup him in my palm.

"My body wants you, but that's all. I'll come in my hand until I have to fulfill the damn prophecy." He crowds me again, his nose skating along my throat. "You don't deserve my tongue or my cock. You don't deserve to come. You've done nothing to earn it."

"So bringing you back to life doesn't count? Fine. I'll just use my hand too."

He tangles his hand in my hair and tilts my face. "No you won't. This is the first part of your punishment. The wanting. You're not allowed to touch yourself. Not even a graze. I forbid it. I'll know if you do. My beast will smell it. And we'll punish you." He reaches down and pulls the jeans up. "Sweet dreams, witch."

He throws me a smugly evil smile over his shoulder and leaves me hanging there. I'm wrinkled and twisted. On the inside and the outside. I want to shove my hand into my pants and finish what he began. Surely, he's lying. If I soak in the baths, he'll never know I disobeyed him.

Should I take the risk? Is it worth the punishment that will follow? What if the punishment is more of this? Or less of it? Or something else altogether?

A kiss, perhaps. I miss the satin slide of his lips against mine.

I steel myself against the insistent throb. I'm going to think of him every time I take a step. Maybe I can ignore it if Meghan loans me one of her monster romance books as a distraction.

Chapter Twenty-Nine

Eachann

Callum is only too eager to divest himself of the crown. One meeting with the vizier was all it took to schedule the ceremony.

Three days later I'm standing here with a ridiculous pink silk pillow (Sabh handed it to me with a smirk) that holds the ritual dagger.

I'm focusing on the vizier's liver-spotted hands so I won't look at her. We all turned when the herald announced her arrival and the impact of her in that dress almost brought me to my knees. I'm going to ignore the shimmer of red fabric molded to her breasts.

I knew she'd be wearing red because my great aunt is a stickler for tradition. But I didn't expect it to be such a deep dark red her hair is the color of blood against it. I keep my gaze fixed on the vizier and the brehons that flank him instead of the flash of bare leg that taunts me as she saunters in my direction. I am oblivious to the defiant tilt of her jaw and the luscious temptation of her lips and the scent of musk and orange blossom that wafts from her skin as she approaches.

I haven't touched or tasted her since I manipulated her in the library. I've fallen asleep every night with my hand around my cock and my eyes and mind weary from absorbing Duncan's binders full of notes and data. If I'm exhausted, I'm not tempted to seek her out.

"We are gathered here to sanctify the union between our king and his chosen mate. This is their official coronation and sigil ceremony." The pompous announcement is a call to order and the hubbub of noise fades away. All eyes are glued on us.

The vizier signals Callum to step forward. My brother's stride is fleet and he's placing the crown on the pillow before he's even prompted to do so.

"Good riddance! It's all yours, older brother!" He claps me on the shoulder and assumes his place in the front row beside Meghan.

I kneel before the vizier so he can place it on my brow. As soon as I feel the weight of it, everything I am called to do in the name of duty overwhelms me. I don't know how my father did it, or how Callum bore standing in for me.

When I rise, I feel changed. And resentful. My life will never again be my own.

I place the blade in the palm of my mate's hand and her gaze fastens on mine with grim determination. I bend near when she lets the tip rest against my skin and makes no move to perform the ritual. "Do it, witch. This time my blood will be spilt by your own hands instead of those who spill it at your behest."

She bites her lip and hesitantly nicks my skin. I place my hands over hers and press closer. Her eyes widened in alarm when the metal pierces my skin. When I drop my head and swallow her gasp, her muscles quiver and tense in protest. "Do it, witch." I repeat. "Carve your mark into my skin as I will carve mine into yours. Let us seal this bargain."

"Fine," she mutters.

She tightens her grasp on the hilt and leans in. Her touch is no longer tentative. It is sure and swift and precise as she fully leashes my beast. She drops the bloodied knife on the pillow one of the brehons now holds.

Before she can step away, I press her head to my chest. "Not yet. You must finish the job. Lick the wound clean."

She shudders with revulsion.

"You'll not quarrel with me in this. Put your sharp tongue to good use."

"Would that I could flay you with it for this humiliation."

"It is the way of our kind. I already know you are a bloodthirsty wench, so set aside this pretense of disgust and obey me."

I cup her nape and push her head inexorably down.

The first lap of her tongue is as hesitant as her first prick of the blade. She grows more confident as the blood wells, and there's no mistaking the purring sound she makes when her teeth scrape against the ruched skin. It hardens to a bead beneath the stroke of her tongue and I don't bother disguising my groan. She lifts her head.

"Retribution tastes sweet, prince."

She's exacting vengeance for my refusal to let her reach satisfaction. "King, not prince." I correct. "And now it is my turn for retribution."

I pick up the dagger, wipe it clean of my blood against the leg of my trousers, and straighten her arm. My cuts are even more swift and precise than hers. I carve my each uisge name into her skin. Amhran de Cogadh, War Song. When the blood wells, I lift her wrist to my mouth.

Her blood tastes like the emerald of leaves. Like moss and vetiver. I slip the leather from my wrist to hers, so it staunches her blood.

I felt the tremor when I grasped her elbow and know she bit the inside of her cheek to keep from straining against my hold. My savage satisfaction isn't dimmed by her reluctance.

I drop her arm and wrap her shoulders to draw her close. "These are the sigils of my house and the sigil of my each uisge name. My each uisge is Amhran de Cogadh. Learn it. I am bound to come to your aid if you touch the mark on your wrist and say his name three times."

We have no time for celebrations. I'm fully launching my campaign for revenge and the first battle begins tonight. I weave my way through the crowd, dragging her behind me. I ignore the way she stumbles in my grasp, and I'm too angry to care if my hold is too tight. I finished setting up the interrogation room yesterday. Everyone is under the mistaken impression we're going to my keep for our honeymoon. We're not. We're going there because I'm finally going to get her to admit what she did.

I think the only ones I haven't fooled are Meghan and Callum.

One of the first things my brother did when he assumed the throne was restore the ruins of the fortress I started building for my mate and I before I was killed. He told me it was still mostly unfurnished when he handed me the keys, but he doubted we'd leave the bed much anyway.

I didn't correct him.

We won't be using a bed and I'm still torturing her. I can't believe she actually obeyed me. She smells of constant arousal, but it has the brimstone edge of frustration. I know she hasn't given herself release. I don't know how long I'll withhold it, but I like having her at my mercy.

It's a short ride to our destination and Carrig volunteered to chauffeur us there because cars are only one of the many modern conveniences I haven't learned to use. He drives a huge truck, but it's still almost too small for the three of us. My mate is squeezed between us, her nose nearly smashed into my armpit.

When the castle comes into view, I feel my new bride tense beside me. As soon as we're standing in the circular drive, Carrig salutes me and peels off in a spray of gravel, laying on his horn. If I'd bound myself to any other woman, I'd be amused by his antics.

But because my bride is her, I'm not amused.

I grasp her upper arm in one hand and extract the ring of keys from my pocket with the other.

I don't bother giving her a tour. She's going to be confined to a single room.

When I stop in front of the heavy metal door, she balks. "What is this? A vault?"

"Yes. A vault to keep you from causing trouble. A vault where you'll spill your truths."

She struggles in my grip and I laugh. "I've been planning this for weeks, mate."

Her eyes widen when I swing open the door. The room is part of the original keep. The walls are rough, gray stone, and there are no windows. There's a chair in the middle of it with ropes dangling from the arms and spindles. There's nothing else.

She struggles even harder, but it's to no avail. She's no match for me. I throw her in the chair and bracket her throat with my hand. "I'll never forgive you for your betrayal." I tell her before I take the gag from my other pocket and tie it tight under the heavy weight of her hair.

I tie her hands together behind the chair. When I move to her ankles, she tries to strike out at me. I smack her thigh and shake my head in warning.

I leave her there. Tied up and fuming on her wedding night. I smile as I fall into the most restful sleep I've had since she called me back from the Otherworld.

Chapter Thirty

Galanta

I don't know what sort of treatment I expected from him. But it wasn't this. Not from the man who once vowed to protect me with his sword and shield. The nerves in my hands and feet tingle from disuse, and my neck and shoulders are stiff from the laddered back of the chair I was forced to curl into if I wanted to sleep.

My stomach has been growling in protest the last hour, and my mouth is dry.

I stretch my limbs as far as I can against my bindings and dream about a full breakfast of waffles and coffee and orange juice. (Meghan is obsessed with waffles, and she's slowly converting me to her cause).

I'm trying to decide if I'd rather have blueberries or strawberries slathered on top of my imaginary breakfast when the door slams open.

He stalks toward me.

"You betrayed me. You lured me to that cove and wrought the destruction of my kingdom and the death of my parents. You rendered me vulnerable and I will never again act the fool."

"I had no knowledge of what my family and the priest had planned for you."

"They could not have known of our assignation unless you told them. They heard it from your lips. Your deceitful, treacherous lips."

He bends his head and clenches my bottom lip between his teeth hard enough to draw blood. "You owe me the blood that was shed on your behalf."

I lick the drop of blood away and his gaze fastens on that slight movement, like a wolf that's scented its prey. "I owe you nothing." I haughtily reply. "All I ever gave you was my heart. And I feel the loss of years as deeply as you. I wanted our babe. I wanted you. There is no debt between us."

"Should I make you prove it?"

His hands move to the waistband of the loose sweatpants barely disguising his tented arousal. I lick my lips in anticipation. I may be pathetic for wanting this, but I'll take even this twisted, false scrap of lust masquerading as affection.

"I'd like to see you try."

His eyes flare at my challenge, and he yanks the pants down to his thighs. "Once upon a time, I dreamt about feeding this to you slowly." He strokes his length to emphasize his words. "But now I want to scrape against your throat until you choke. Until you're full of nothing but me and the taste of my cock, leannan."

The endearment is a revelation. He may claim he feels nothing but hatred, but if that was all he felt, he wouldn't call me beloved. He's yet to call me his wild heart, but when he does, I'll know this war between us is at an end.

He's fully erect, and a bead of his semen glistens at the tip. I've never tasted him. Even our tryst in the hay was too brief for us to linger over anything but the most essential union. I want to taste him now. I want to rasp my tongue along every heavy ridge of that ruddy, hard cock. I'll gladly choke on it.

"That's not a threat, mo stoirm." I hear the rough scrape of need in my voice.

His gaze narrows at the reminder of what we were before, but he doesn't acknowledge it beyond that single slip of his composure. His hand slowly slides down his length, his wrist flexing as he tugs and tosses his head back.

My golden prince is anything but indifferent to me, and I wonder if his beast is roaring in his chest right now. Does his beast think I betrayed them as well? Or is he more understanding than his obstinate, maddening other half?

"According to Sabhinion, you are the key to saving my kingdom. Once I plant my seed in you again, I'll have no qualms about sacrificing you to the sea as punishment for your treason."

I lower my gaze. His strokes are tighter now, almost punishing.

"You can plow me later," I taunt. "Right now I want nothing more than the taste of you on my tongue."

He groans. "Then you'll swallow me down, witch."

No endearment this time.

He stomps angrily forward, his hand still clasped around his cock. He swipes his thumb over the head and works his cum into his skin as he viciously tugs it again. As soon as he's near my mouth, I lean forward.

My hands are tied behind my back, my ankles trussed together. The angle of my body as I lean in makes my breasts feel tender and full. He paints the drop of cum on his thumb over my bottom lip and presses my mouth open.

He thrusts inside and fists his hands in my hair as he scrapes along the roof of my mouth and bottoms out.

I want him to touch me, but I'm not going to beg. I may be at his mercy, but he's not in the mood to show it. He exhales and swells impossibly larger. My body flexes as my throat constricts around his girth.

I watch him as my tongue laves every ridge it can reach, and he shudders in response.

"Fu-u-u-u-u-ck!" He bellows. And then one possessive hand lands on my breast, twisting my nipple as he pistons his hips. I suck hard, like I want to steal the breath from his body, and he loses all control.

"Ye damned witch, I cannae hold back." The cant of the islands lets me know he's on the verge of losing control. I swirl my tongue over every single ridge and that's all it takes. He coats my throat and I swallow until he's empty. When I rear back, his semen dribbles down my chin. He covers his fingers with it and strums my bottom lip again. "Lick them clean, leannan."

I do. Because I want to watch his eyes glitter even more with each sinuous flick of my tongue.

He's silent when I finish, but his chest is heaving and his cock is already at half-mast. I gaze at it pointedly, so he knows exactly what I'm focused on. "Witch," he murmurs.

It doesn't sound like an insult this time. It sounds like an endearment. A new one as he wryly shakes his head and swipes a hand across his face.

He moves away, but he doesn't leave. He grabs a bottle of water that still has condensation sliding down its sides. I close my eyes as he holds it against my forehead. I bite my lip and moan when he coasts it down the side of my neck.

My breasts are still heavy and aching, my nipples taut and furled with how much I need his touch and tongue and teeth. He rolls the chilled bottle over the beaded tips and I hiss in response.

He tortures me with that damn bottle. It's the only thing he's going to let touch my skin because he's back in control. "I'm going to leave you just like this. If I do anything else, it will be a reward. And even though you were a good lass and swallowed my cock like you were born for it, you don't deserve a reward. The one concession I'm going to make is your wrists. If your circulation suffers, you won't be able to use your hands on me later. And I need your hands on me." He grabs a tin of something from the narrow shelf mounted to the wall and moves behind the chair.

He unties me and I whimper at the tingling in my hands when he frees them. He lifts them up and I swear I feel the brush of his rough satin lips against my bruised knuckles.

And then he's rubbing something into the welts on my wrists in a steady, circular motion. Whatever it is brings instant relief and I sigh in contentment. I smell menthol and olive, and something else I cannot place. My herbalist palate tries to parse out the other ingredients.

"Though I've untied your hands, you'll take your night's rest in this chair," he rumbles behind me.

He drops one of his hooded sweatshirts across my shoulders and I shrug it on, grateful for that small bit of warmth that carries his scent.

"There's a cinnamon roll in the pocket." He mumbles over his shoulder as he slams through the door again.

I'm probably a fool, but the sweatshirt I just shrugged into and the cinnamon roll I extract and lift to my lips, give me hope.

Chapter Thirty-One

Eachann

How could I have forgotten the effect she has on me? My soul was drifting for millennia, plotting how I would master her. Our first true night together and she has mastered me. She still has the power to destroy me with those leaf green eyes and ripe berry lips that taste like sunlight. I won't kiss her. As much as I want to. Because kissing is how we began. How I became insatiable for her. How I fell so hard and so fast I lost my heart on the way down.

I will tease her. And then let her wither. I want to cast aside this unwieldy tenderness too, and let it wither. She doesn't deserve it.

I shouldn't be giving her cinnamon rolls or letting her borrow my clothes.

There's a knock on the door, and my new sister-in-law peeks her head around the edge.

She opens her mouth and I know she's going to chastise me for what she thinks is harsh behavior. She and Galanta became friends while they were looking for a way to outmaneuver the prophecy.

I hold up a hand to halt whatever plea she's come to make. "No. I am the king and her liege. I will let none gainsay me in my treatment of her."

Not my brother. And especially not this woman who wears her heart on her sleeve – even when she's full of nothing but tart sarcasm. Her sympathy is misplaced.

"None of what happened is her fault," Meghan protests.

"I have seen no proof of that. I only know that she arranged our last meeting. Instead of accompanying me after her rescue, she made some paltry excuse about retrieving something precious. Something too dear to leave behind. She stumbled into her infernal woods and I let her go. When I returned, I was ambushed and murdered. She has much to answer for and a debt of blood to pay."

"Even Callum is beginning to believe she's innocent. And we both known he's the most skeptical man alive."

"You have softened my brother. When we were young, he would have been the last person to believe her lies or accept her alibis. He would have fed her to the wild kraken himself."

She wags a finger in my face. "You know that's untrue. Fatherhood may have softened him, but he's still formidable. Mal and Mabh have just given him the grace to see both sides of a story. You loved this woman once. How can you so easily dismiss her?"

"The love I once held is the reason I dismiss her. She broke my trust. She has a way of burrowing under my defenses, and I cannot allow her to do it again. I let her in and she destroyed everything I loved."

A wide hand lands on Meghan's shoulder and Callum's head suddenly looms in the doorway.

"Is my wife haranguing you again, brother?"

"She is. She wants me to be more merciful toward my prisoner."

"Your prisoner that is now also your consecrated mate and wears your sigil." He steps into the room, my newborn niece cradled in his arms. My nephew is wrapped around one his legs and giggles when he feigns shaking him loose. I turn my head to hide how much their antics affect me.

"My prisoner." I grit out the contradiction.

"From what Callum's told me, she had nothing to do with your betrayal. She was not in the confidence of her family." Meghan seems assured of this.

"She may not have been until they captured her. She orchestrated my downfall to save her own skin. There is no other feasible explanation."

"Why would she do that? You were the father of her child and she'd already given her heart to you."

"She could not remain steadfast. She bared our secrets to her kin."

She watches me carefully. "I think you're wrong, Eachann. I think she did everything she could to protect you."

"You were never one to hold grudges, brother. Especially unfounded ones." Callum chides me.

I ignore the censure in his tone. "There is no one else it could have been. No one with that knowledge."

"You've jumped to conclusions and found her guilty without bothering to consider any other scenario. Just like they did when they accused her of witchcraft. You claim to have loved her once, but your treatment of her is no better than theirs."

After launching her vehement condemnation, Meghan whirls about and extracts the children from Callum before she stomps away.

My brother crosses his arms and narrows his eyes to scrutinize me. I refuse to squirm beneath his regard.

"You were never the hard, unforgiving one. That was me. You forgave and forgot and learned from your mistakes. I always admired that about you. But you've changed. You're bitter and broken. And unreachable."

I glare at him. "How would you react if you'd watched yourself being drawn and quartered and shoved into the cold ground far away from the cradle of the sea?"

"But you didn't stay there." He points out. "You're only standing here because she risked her life to entomb you properly. You wouldn't be here now if not for her. Why would she do that, risk that, if she had a hand in your murder?"

"You'll not change my mind, brother. Once she bears my child, she'll take my place beneath the water. And the prophecy will be fulfilled."

"So now Sabh thinks it's about you."

"I think she's right. I am the true heir. And I'm willing to make this sacrifice to protect our kingdom."

"Duncan doesn't think it will make a difference. He says the water is warming and that's why we are in danger. That all of the uncertainty we face is because of the rise of mortal technology."

"Mortal technology we have embraced since I've been gone."

Callum scowls. "That's all courtesy of Cairneach and Creiddylad's rule. Good riddance to their influence."

"But you made no changes in your brief reign."

"The way our kind lives now is too entrenched. Our power and wealth gave us more freedom than we've ever had to move about the world. The each uisge do not want to give up their private jets and Caribbean getaways."

"We must become more circumspect. How has our presence remained undiscovered?"

He shrugs. "Mortals no longer believe in the supernatural. Especially tales of the fae. Any encounter is written off as a hallucination or a dream. Or what they call cosplay. They believe they are alone in their dominion over the natural world."

"Is this what the prophecy foresaw? A world without our kind or magic?"

"In a way. Sabh thinks it foresaw the collapse of our kingdom and the end of our way of life. According to her, fulfilling the prophecy is the only solution."

"Our sister has been wrong about many things."

"She has. But I don't think she's wrong about this."

"Then I guess it's a good thing I'm back. You love your mate. I do not love mine. Her death by sacrifice is what she deserves for her treachery."

"I'll stop trying to convince you otherwise for now. I think you'll convince yourself as her womb grows heavy with your seed."

He closes the door firmly behind him and I curse under my breath. I need to be the cold of winter where she's concerned.

Chapter Thirty-Two

Galanta

He torments me at every opportunity. Every time I feel his breath against my neck or his grip on my wrist, I harden my resolve. My resistance is pointless and always amounts to nothing.

He didn't take me to my dungeon tonight. Instead, my ankles are tied to the chair in his bedroom.

He turned me so I'm facing the mirror, fully exposed. Of course he's fully dressed. The long sleeves of his dress shirt are rolled neatly to the elbow and it's unbuttoned nearly to his navel, so the runes on his chest are on peekaboo display.

"Your hands are free, witch."

"Yes." My eyes seek out his in the reflection.

"I want them on me. But not yet."

I want my hands on him too. And his on me.

"How should I occupy myself in the meantime?"

"You're going to show me how you want me to touch you when I finally show you mercy."

He's been edging me for weeks. "I grow weary of this game."

He steps behind me and grips my chin. "It's not a game, witch. This is your punishment."

I close my eyes. If I barely touch myself, I can hold off my orgasm. I hope. "Fine."

I slide my finger through my folds and when my eyes flutter open, his gaze is feral.

"Good lass," he growls. And then he unzips his slacks.

He's not wearing anything beneath them, and his cock bobs toward his stomach. He wraps a fist around the base and tugs, just like he did in the dungeon room. There's something about watching him do it through the mirror that makes it even more provocative.

"Spread those gorgeous petals, lass. Let me see how wet you are."

I don't do it for him. Not entirely. I do it because he looks like he's going to throw me over his shoulder and finally end my misery.

I glide my fingers over my clit and my entire body twitches in response. His pace speeds up and he grunts.

"I want to come, Eachann."

"We've already discussed it. You'll come when I say you can come."

"Please."

I want the release so much it's painful.

"Nay. More begging."

He steps closer. His cock is even with my head, and every time he tugs it from the base it grazes my cheek.

"I think you're suffering too. I think you're lying when you tell me your hand is enough."

"My hand is enough." He rumbles in my ear. "But tonight, I crave more."

He raises my hand and sucks my fingers clean. "Someday I'll taste you again, leannan."

"Someday?"

"Someday. Not today. Not tonight. Tonight, you'll show me untying your hands wasn't a lapse of judgment."

He lifts me into his arms and carries me to the bed. "Kneel, so you're facing the mirror."

I warily obey.

He kneels behind me, his thighs bracketing mine. I can feel the length of him pulsing against my back. "Put my hands where you want them."

I lift one to my breast and slide the other one down my stomach.

"How rough do you want it, leannan?"

His slip gives me hope. When he's unguarded and craving me, I am more than a witch to him. "Surprise me."

His palm hovers over my navel, his eyes bright and hard in the reflection.

"You asked for it."

The sharp smack makes my clitoris throb. It stings, and I want to move away or tell him enough and too much, but then my eyes catch his in the mirror again. The way he's wrapped around me makes my heart flutter, and instead of leaning away from him, I arch backward and scoot closer.

"Remember. You're not allowed to come."

I bite my lip and nod at his fierce warning.

He does it again. My body quakes in response and I can't hold back the moan that's climbing my throat.

I'm plastered against him, balanced on my feet, and I feel them flex between us. He slides his nose down my throat and closes his teeth over the tendon. I thrash my head against his shoulder and he smacks me again.

"You're so unfair..." I moan.

"All is fair in love and war, witch. And this is war."

It doesn't feel like war. It feels like we're burning something down so we can rise from its ashes.

"This might be a battle, husband, but it's not part of a war. You are not my enemy."

"But you are mine." He strokes my breast before he tugs it to a hard point and feathers his fingers through my curls before he thrusts them inside.

I keen at the exquisite pressure and buck against him.

"You are easily tamed."

He lifts his hands from me and that's the end of tonight's torture session. Every particle of my body is thrumming and blazing. Like it does every night.

"I am not a wild creature you need to tether and control."

"You are the wildest of creatures, witch. Designed to ensorcel the unsuspecting and lead them to their deaths."

"Your bitterness is misdirected and will eventually poison everything you touch. I'm sleeping on the floor."

"Suit yourself, witch. I'll be merciful."

He tosses me one of the blankets.

I would be warmer in the bed, because his body is like a furnace. But I cannot bear to be close to him. To feel his touch and his breath and know it springs from nothing but loathing.

I wrap myself in the quilt and fall asleep.

Chapter Thirty-Three

Eachann

She slipped outside after dinner. She comes out here every night and braces her elbows on the stone wall. Arms crossed; expression forlorn. Every night I follow her. Because I cannot stay away. Some nights I make her bend at the waist, so her hair's swirling in the breeze and covering her face. Other nights I cage her with my body and make her show me how she likes to be touched. When she's gasping and looking up at me with those green velvet eyes, I almost hear the music.

My favorite nights are the ones full of torment. When I fuck her slowly with my hands and mouth and walk away before she comes. Those are the nights I love the most because she's completely at my mercy. She's not allowed to finish what I start, and bringing her to the edge and leaving her so dazed she's flushed and stuttering and teetering on her feet, barely able to stand is glorious.

I haven't asked why she comes out here. If it's for herself or if it's an invitation.

Maybe she comes out here because she misses her forest, and the tree line is visible in the distance. Or maybe she comes out here because she's at least three hundred feet above the ground and the sky is closer. She said the breeze through her feathers was the only thing she missed from her time as one of Morrigan's couriers.

I cage her in front of me and she sighs. "I knew I couldn't escape you. Is this how we're always going to be?"

"What do you mean?"

"Are you ever going to forgive me? Are you ever going to finish what you start?"

"At least you're not tied up in my interrogation room."

She snorts. "Small mercies. I might as well be stuck in that cold, dark room again by myself."

"That can be arranged."

She whirls to face me, her eyes wild. She's been crying. "Why can't you see me? It's still me. Your green girl, your wild heart. Thousands of years may have passed, but that never changed."

She may be the same, but I'm not. A darkness twists inside me that wasn't there before. Even when I feasted and drank mead in the Otherworld, it was there. Even when I hold my niece and nephew, it's there. I can't push it away, no matter what I do. It's been there since I lost the music again. I don't think I'll ever get it back because my music came from joy. And joy is something foreign to me now.

I haven't kissed her because I don't want to let her in. I don't want her to sense that core of darkness that's slowly eviscerating me from the inside out. But maybe her kiss is the key to banishing it forever.

I drop my lips to hers and she tenses. But only for the time it takes her to inhale. Then her arms are around my neck, tugging me down and molding me closer. She hums into the kiss and that tiny sign of appreciation tips me over the edge. I lift her to the wall and she locks her ankles at the base of my spine. I'm always behind her, so she hasn't felt me against her like this since our last time in the glade. When her tongue traced over every single rune.

I surge forward as our tongues tangle together. She tastes just as I remember. "The berries..." I murmur into the kiss. She pulls away. "They put them in jam now. I slather it on my toast every morning."

"Never stop," I tell her before I dive back in. I scrape my teeth over her tongue, and swallow the hoarse cry she makes when I bite her bottom lip.

I'm so arrested by the kiss; the slice of the knife doesn't register.

She'll always be the instrument of my tragedy.

I feel her hands slide away and hear her screaming. I have the fleeting thought that if I'd not been so enthralled by the sweet bow of her lips, I would have thwarted the assassin's blade before it struck.

The last thing I see before I lose consciousness is her. She's standing in front of me, her hands outstretched. Wind is tunneling around her, and vines climb her bared legs. She's covered in bright green light.

When I wake up, I know she's been here. Her scent lingers in the air – like rain falling on leaves. I remember how she tasted. Like she snatched a handful of berries from the bramble again. A single, scarlet strand of hair snakes across the pillow.

There's a perfunctory knock and my brother strides in. "You're lucky your mate was there when it happened."

"She's what distracted me so I was vulnerable to attack."

"She's the one who saved you. Her power finally showed itself."

I swing my feet to the floor and brace my elbows on my knees. The pucker of skin from the stitches pulls tight with the movement and I wince.

"How will you deal with this? An assassin never should have crept through our defenses."

"You're the warlord. What do you suggest?"

"This is not war. This is cowardice. Setting a target on a man's back in his own home."

"It has to be one of our uncle's cronies."

"We have many enemies, brother. Mayhap it's someone who doesn't want the prophecy to be fulfilled. Especially if it means our kingdom will prosper."

"Does Riordan have any leads?"

"No. But Carrig thinks his father might be behind it."

"Since when does the Kraken King care about the Each Uisge Realm? Aren't we what your mate calls small potatoes compared to his vast domain?"

"Maybe this is how he gets his son's attention."

"That doesn't make sense. Carrig has never said anything, but if his father reached out, I don't think he'd turn him away. He has no one left but us."

"He's more bitter since his father's enemy kidnapped his sister."

"When we rescued her, none of us knew how damaged she was by what she went through."

"He blames himself. He's blamed himself for two thousand years and nothing any of us says or does will convince him there's nothing he could have done to prevent any of it from happening."

"That still doesn't explain why he thinks his father's behind my attack."

"Because whoever your attacker was, they dropped their weapon. And the knife hilt carried the seal of the kraken warrior guild. Not to mention the fact your mate said it was dipped in kraken venom."

"Kraken venom is deadly."

"Yes. And my green magic that you despise was the only thing that saved you." My mate defiantly says as she steps into the room.

"I never said I despised it."

"Last night was our first kiss in almost two thousand years."

"I don't think I'm needed here. It sounds like the two of you have some things to work out." Callum strides away with a grin he doesn't bother hiding.

I scowl at the closed door. "I've never despised you," I mutter.

She sits on the bed beside me. "It feels like you do."

"I don't despise you. I despise myself. For still wanting you so desperately. Like swords and death never came between us. For still remembering the way your skin feels and how you taste. For how much you haunt me when all I want to do is forget that any of it happened."

"Any of it? Don't you mean all of it?"

"Any of it. All of it. The words don't matter."

"Nothing matters but the words. Because you won't give them to me. You won't talk about what happened to you in the Otherworld. Or why you're so bitter."

"I have every reason to be bitter. Every reason to cherish my resentment and loathing."

She picks at a loose thread in the quilt. "And you think I don't? Some people say the true enemy of love is apathy, not hatred."

"Yes. Some people say that."

She raises her chin. "Maybe you still love me and that's why you're so angry."

"I think you're mistaking your feelings for my own."

"I never stopped loving you, Eachann. I gave up everything for you. And when I finally atoned for all my mistakes, you threw my love in my face and treated me like nothing more than a vessel."

Chapter Thirty-Four

Galanta

The nights in the interrogation room ended weeks ago. But the torment didn't. He had a ritual of making me beg every night on the balcony. That stopped too after the kiss. After he was beholden because I called on my magic to save him.

He still ties my feet together at the beginning of each night. He usually unties me once he's made me a quivering mess. When I asked why, he gave me one of his inscrutable looks and said, "So you won't run."

Why would I run, I'd wanted to scream. *I have nowhere to go and no one to run to but you, and you can barely tolerate me.*

He hasn't said anything about my confession. He hasn't even thanked me for saving his life. I don't know what I expected when I brought him back, but I know it wasn't this.

I'm tired of being the object of blame for every tragic thing that happened to him. Tragic things happened to me as well. But I've never wallowed in them. I used them to forge me into something stronger. Something that can withstand anything.

I'm curled on my side, my hands tucked beneath my cheek, my bound feet pointed so my toes won't go numb, when I feel his touch on my ankles.

"What are you doing?"

"Filling my vessel."

I snap my eyes open, the morning bleariness gone. "What?" I croak.

"You heard me."

He pulls me up and leads me to the wall. When I'm facing it, he positions my hands so they're splayed flat, just above my shoulders. He kicks my legs apart and I feel his hot breath on my nape. I shiver in response and he growls before clenching the tender skin of my earlobe in his teeth. My body sways backward and bumps against his arousal.

"Teasing, taunting witch," he hisses.

He hasn't let me have underwear since the library incident. I sleep in the worn hooded sweatshirt he threw at me after he came in my mouth.

It barely skims the top of my thighs and my nipples pebble behind the soft fabric. I lie to myself and attribute it to the breeze coming in through the open window instead of the man at my back.

He slides his fingers under the edge of the leather cuff that encircles my wrist. "Mine." He bites my nape again.

"Am I?" I gasp.

"Aye. Since that first day when I leaned through your open window."

I bite my lip against the words rising behind my tongue. I will not ask.

"I can feel you seething. Tell me why." His hand slides under the hem of the shirt.

"What I say will make no difference."

"How will you know unless you say?"

"You'll not leave it be."

"No."

"I want to know why you haven't kissed me since that night."

He hasn't kissed me again. Not since the night he was attacked. But he knows every inch of my body. Even more intimately than he did the first time we fell in love. He knows exactly how to bring me to the edge.

He never pushes me over. Or goes there with me.

I've never fallen out of love with him, and I sense he's finally softening toward me. I want him to kiss me. I've been afraid to ask. Afraid to risk capsizing the fragile truce between us. Afraid if I ask I'll find myself in the interrogation room again. Shivering and bound to a chair with nothing but my thoughts for company.

The hand that was stroking my ribs stills on my skin. Gooseflesh rises beneath the heat of his palm.

"I can't kiss you. If I kiss you, I'll forget why you deserve to be punished."

"What will it take to convince you of my innocence?"

"Produce another explanation. Another culprit. That is the only thing that will convince me."

"You know that's impossible. Whoever betrayed you is long dead, their bones nothing more than dust. How was your trust in me so fragile that you would believe me capable of turning you over to them?"

"You were not the first woman to betray me."

"Did our vows to each other mean nothing? You swore your sword as my protection, your cloak as my shelter. You gave me the wild heart of your beast."

His sigh coasts over me as he drops his head and kisses my shoulder. "I did."

"And you swore it again here, in this time and place."

He drops a kiss on the opposite shoulder. "I did."

"So you meant it both times?"

This time his kiss lands on my first vertebra. "I did."

"Then why won't you kiss me on the mouth?"

"You know why. Because when I kiss you, you'll hold the final piece of my heart again. And I'll lose all sense of my surroundings. So much I won't hear assassins."

His lips gloss over the skin just under my shoulder blades.

"So you won't kiss me because you're afraid. Just to be clear, assassins are trained to be silent and deadly. Your sister-in-law would say it's literally in their job description. I didn't hear the assassin either."

"No. You failed to perform your duty as my shield and cloak."

I feel his smile against my skin. The first true one I've felt since he returned.

"As I recall, my vow was to accept the shield and cloak you offered. Not provide one in return."

"Uncharitable, witch."

There's no mistaking the feel of his smile against me this time.

"I will show you charity when I know it will be returned."

He sets his hand at my waist and turns me into his arms. "It will be returned. Even though I'm afraid, I'll return it."

The kiss begins with a sigh. His hands cradle my jaw and hold me captive and his lips feather across mine like wings. This is the first time I've felt an echo of the man he once was.

"Finally," I murmur. I lift my hands to his face and cup the broad planes of his cheeks with my palms. When my fingers slide into the dark blond waves of his hair, he pushes me flat against the wall.

"Leannan. I didn't want to believe any of it. But I couldn't help myself."

"Is this an apology?"

"Aye. At least I'm trying to make it one. As you know, apologizing isn't one of my strengths."

"You have other ones that make up for the lack. As long as you eventually repent."

"I'm repenting now, mate. For the way I've treated you since I returned."

"Are you repenting for making me wait?"

He slides his nose up my throat and his shoulders shake with laughter. "I'm not apologizing for that. I enjoyed making you wait."

"I didn't enjoy it." I grumble.

"Anticipation makes the reward all the sweeter. And I know how sweet your cunt can be, mo chridhe fiadhaich."

"Finally."

"Finally what?"

"You're finally calling me that again."

"Aye, my wild heart with her sweet cunny and smart mouth." He brackets my wrists above my head with one hand and anchors my leg around his waist with the other.

I moan at the tight fit when he slides his fingers in. I moan again when he removes them and lifts them to his mouth, glittering, feral eyes on me the whole time as he licks them clean.

"Sweet." He presses open mouthed kisses over the dip between my breasts. "Sweet everywhere. But I want you to fuck more than my fingers and tongue this time."

I reach between us and scrape my nails down his length. He throws his head back. "Wee witch. Put me inside you."

I clasp the tight globe of his ass and pull him toward me. We both gasp when he sinks in all the way to the hilt. "Thank the goddess you got tired of waiting too."

"I never wanted to wait, mate. But the last time I gave you all of me, you shattered it. You'll understand my reluctance to give you so much power again."

"You have the same power over me. I didn't seek out the spell to repent for the past. I sought it out because I wanted you, wanted this. Wanted us. Because even then, we never truly had an us. Just stolen moments. Despite the prophecy looming over our lives, I want an us. Let's please have an us this time."

My throat is hoarse and I feel the tears sliding down my cheeks. He kisses them away as he begins to move inside me. I've been on the verge of coming for weeks. He's been bringing me to the very edge and leaving me to stave off the hunger.

He cups my nape and angles my head down. "Watch, leannan. Watch what you do to me. How you make my beast want to spend the day hammering you into this wall."

His slides into me again, excruciatingly slow. I feel every ridge scrape against me, and lean into the hands cusping my throat and my hip.

My foot twitches when he bottoms out. It twitches again when he fists the hair at my nape.

When he sucks my earlobe into his mouth and I feel his teeth, it twitches.

When he strokes his thumb over my clit as he thrusts home again, it twitches.

When he does all four and says, "Come for me, wife." I detonate into a thousand shards of oblivion. I'm floating and weightless somewhere, and I never want to relinquish this feeling. I can feel the spread of the wings that live within me, and my green magic sparks along my veins.

Chapter Thirty-Five

Eachann

There's nothing in my heart but the weight of her in my arms. I want to take back all of my angry words.

"I'm sorry, mo chridhe fiadhaich."

I feel her body tense against mine and watch as her shoulders become visibly rigid. I'm spooned against her, my arms around her waist and my nose in her loose curls.

"I should have known this was just a temporary lapse in your judgment."

Her voice is hollow, and the bitterness in her tone makes me even more aware of how unfair I've been. I turn her around so our legs are tangled and we're face to face. She closes her eyes when I tilt her chin up. As if she is afraid of what she will see in my eyes.

"Open your eyes and look at me."

"Why? I can't bear to look at you right now. Not when I thought everything was fixed between us and I was wholly yours again. Knowing it wasn't, that you regret it, is making everything inside me shatter."

Her confession is ragged with the edge of tears – and it breaks my heart anew. I once vowed to destroy anyone who hurt her, and I've broken that vow in the worst way possible. "Open your eyes, leannan."

She does. But then squeezes them shut again, her tears a crystal path escaping the flutter of her lashes. "You misunderstand me. I am sorry for the way I've treated you since my return. You were not to blame for any of it, but I let my anger and sorrow cloud my judgment." I brush my thumb over her cheeks, wiping away the evidence of the hurt I caused her.

"That's why you're apologizing?"

"Yes. Once upon a time I vowed I would die by my own hand before I would ever lift it toward you."

"You didn't lift it toward me."

"No, I did something far worse. My anger added to the burden of pain you already carry."

A muffled sob reverberates between us and she closes her eyes again. "I've carried it alone for so long. I thought your heart would be healed and joyful when I brought you back. But it wasn't. You looked at me with nothing but hatred. Like you wanted to wrap your hands around my neck and toss me over the cliff."

"The thought crossed my mind. Do you know what my last thought was before your kin slaughtered me on that beach?"

She bites her lip, and I lean forward to catch the drop of scarlet on my tongue.

"I thought of you, leannan. And what a fool I'd been to once again trust the lies of a mortal woman. I did not keep my faith in you or the vows we made."

"You had faith in them then. If you hadn't, you would have let me burn."

"I had faith until your father's blade sliced my throat and your brothers' knives stabbed me in the back."

"Stepfather," she corrects. "He was never my father. He never treated me as a daughter. Only a commodity and a creature to be used and tormented."

"I knew he was the source of your scars. That your relationship was full of enmity and he was naught but a coward. And I still allowed my traitorous past to obscure the truth."

"I resented your anger, but I understood it. You owe me no apologies."

Her generosity of spirit humbles me. "I do. I broke my faith in you. Never again, mo chridhe fiadhaich."

When I caress her cheek, her tears wet my fingers. She's quiet, and my heart hurts for the pain I've caused her since my return. "Do not cry, leannan. I vow only to heal, not harm, for as long as we are together."

My vow is true but rings hollow. Because our time together grows short.

My prickly great-aunt has tears in her eyes. "I thought you were gone forever, dear boy."

Her hands are clamped tightly around the knob of her cane, but I think she wants to clasp one of mine. I place my palm over them.

"How did you escape the carnage, aunt?"

She raises an imperious brow. "Why, blackmail of course. I held too many of your uncle's secrets. And Carrig and Riordan's spy network is made up of my contacts. My great-great-great niece Langihwen is a product of that network."

"The girl you assigned to be my mate's handmaiden?"

My aunt taps her cane on the floor. "She's far more than a handmaiden. Her skills rival those of your best friend and his shadow master. But they are being quite narrow-minded and chauvinistic about using them."

"I can demand they accept her into their ranks."

"No, she needs to convince them on her own. The assignment I just gave her should do the trick. Now," she arranges herself on the settee and picks up her cup and saucer. "Tell me of your adventures."

"I've had no adventures."

She glares at me over the rim of her teacup. "None of my acquaintances who journeyed to the Otherworld have returned. To my knowledge, you are the first ever to do so. Tell me what and who you saw and how you spent your time there."

"The feasts were indescribable. So much bounty. And the woods were full of great stags and wild boar."

"Of course like a typical man the first two things you see fit to describe are food and hunting."

"Well, there was plenty of mead and ale and wine to go with the feast, too," I tease.

"And yet another favorite of each uisge men – libation."

"If I tell you everything about it, will you help us find the assassin?"

"You don't need to bargain with me boy. Especially when you're asking for something I'm already willing to provide. I've already set the wheels in motion."

"So your extensive spy ring is hard at work?"

"At least one of my protegees is."

"Tell me you didn't send Langihwen into a den of vipers."

"I told you, that girl is perfectly capable of taking care of herself. She's far more than she seems. If she'd been in your sister-in-law's chambers the night Cairneach kidnapped her, there would have been no need for an execution. Your sweet cousin would have cut his throat then and there."

"So she is a kitten with claws."

"She bristles with them. Now, finish your story."

Carrig and Callum look at me in disbelief. Riordan's expression is grim.

"She sent who?"

"She sent our cousin. Evidently her handmaiden has an entire arsenal of skills at her disposal."

"She should have left managing the spies to me."

I understand Riordan's anger, but it's misplaced. "If the girl's been trained, which according to our aunt, she has, why are you being so territorial?"

He shoves away from the wall. "I'm not being territorial. This game is not for novices. Whoever attacked you had both the means and opportunity to get past our defenses. That is no small thing - and it means there is a bigger scheme at play. A scheme I'm on the verge of uncovering. I don't want all the groundwork I've laid upset by some half-mad chit with a savior complex."

"I don't think she's half-mad."

He snorts derisively. "Have you had an actual conversation with her?"

"She helped my mate dress for the sigil ceremony."

"That's not a conversation, brother."

"Your brother's right. It's not. She's an insidious, venomous little asp when she wants something."

"You are more well-acquainted with her than the rest of us." It's not a question. His familiarity with our cousin is obvious.

"I was responsible for part of her training."

"When did you find the time for that?" Carrig interjects. "I thought you never had a moment to spare. But if you do, we could use your help training the guards."

"Gladly. Once I intercept your aunt's minion and repair whatever damage she's done."

He gives us all a curt nod before striding out of the room.

Callum expels a whoosh of breath. "That wasn't the reaction we expected."

"No. I think there's more to their acquaintance than training."

Carrig thoughtfully taps his chin. "It's like that song your wife makes you do karaoke to."

Callum groans. "Her obsession with karaoke is the bane of my life. And no, it's not."

"What song?"

"It's called *Another One Bites the Dust.*"

I grin at Carrig's revelation. "It makes sense. I think he was angrier about the possibility of her coming to harm than he was about her involvement."

"You're a fine one to talk." Callum punches him in the arm. "If you ever let our sister get you in a room alone, you're done for."

He vehemently shakes his head. "Not going to happen."

"Someday it will." Sabh is never going to sit back and let him claim anyone but her.

"And when it does, just know that we trust you. You're the only man we'd trust her with. So don't break our trust or her heart." Callum's gaze is friendly, but his grip on our friend's shoulder is white-knuckled.

Carrig glares at the two of us. "Your sister is a pain in my arse."

"That's what you think now. I can't wait to watch your tune change."

Now I'm the sole recipient of his glare. "You'll be waiting a very long time."

"I'm willing to wait. I've gotten quite good at it. But I'm not going to wait for whoever's behind the attempt on my life to try again. Riordan's method of handling it is not the only one there is."

"What do you suggest, brother?" Callum leans forward.

"Carrig, I know you're not going to like this, but I need you to find a contact in your father's court who's willing to speak with you."

He crosses his arms. "You're right. I don't like it. I want nothing to do with my father or his court."

"You're his only heir. Surely someone will talk to you in exchange for the promise of future favors."

"There won't be any future favors. My father's throne can sit empty for eternity once he's gone. I have no intention of assuming it."

"Well, at least make them think you do. It will loosen their tongues."

"You think the Kraken King is behind this?"

"I think it's a very distinct possibility. He's always trying to expand his domain, and his son is already entrenched within our court."

"What if that's where your aunt sent Langihwen?"

I shrug. "What if it is? She'll be disguised. And those she acquires access to will not be those you acquire access to."

"You have no way of knowing that."

"I do. My aunt's web is full of maids and bodyguards and secretaries who begin at the bottom and store secrets until they infiltrate the highest levels of the criminal rings she wants exposed. She collects information and uses it as a weapon for manipulation and blackmail. No one is better at collecting that sort of ammunition than those who are overlooked and taken for granted."

"If I agree to this, you will agree to drop the subject of your sister's obsession. Forever."

"We may drop it for a time, but not forever. Where would the fun be in that? We can't watch you squirm on the hook when she finally gets her way if we agree to that."

I nod. "I agree with my brother. Do this, and we agree to let you wallow in your ignorance for at least a year."

"That's all you're willing to give me in return? A mere twelve months?" He grumbles.

"A year of peace and quiet from our teasing? I thought you'd jump at the chance."

He sticks out his hand. "Fine. I'll do it. But not a word of your sister for at least a year."

Chapter Thirty-Six

Galanta

My eyes flicker open and I gulp in the clean air.
It's not stale or dank. I am not covered in filth.
I am more than skin stretched over bones.

A millennia later I still feel the fetid breath of my gaoler on my neck. I still feel the skitter of rodent claws over my body.

"You had a nightmare," he murmurs at my back.

"How did you know?"

"You were shivering in your sleep, and nothing I did made you warm. Not more coverings, not my arms around you with no space between us. You finally woke when I did this."

He subtly grinds himself against me.

"Likely from irritation at being roused from my dreams." It's not true, but I don't like to think about the way my body always betrays me where he's concerned.

"Those were not the sort of dreams you should surrender yourself to. You needed to wake, mo chridhe."

"You sound certain of that."

"Aye, because I know the sweat of night terrors. The seize of your muscles, the clench of your teeth. Like you will never be safe or warm again."

His lips skate across my shoulders. And then I feel them wisp over the scars on my back. I thought when I turned back from raven to woman, my skin would be unblemished. When I asked, the Morrigan told me those scars had honed my strength and power and were nothing to be ashamed of.

My mate has never seen them in full daylight, until now.

"I would hack every single one of them into pieces if they did not already rot in the ground."

I close my eyes against the feel of his fingertips. The pain has long since faded, but the trace of his callused hands brings the anguish I endured roaring to the surface.

The tears rise from somewhere deep in the pit of my stomach, as if they've been waiting for this.

This is the redemption I sought. His gentle touch on the parts of me that have been broken.

"I am sorry," He mumbles into the curve of my shoulder.

"I bore these wounds before we met."

"Aye, but the way I have treated you since my return has been just as vicious."

"You've already apologized, but I'll not argue with you," I confirm with a sob I desperately try to choke down.

He traces every one of my scars with his mouth and his hands, crooning to me. I fall asleep to him humming beneath his breath, the solid weight of his arm around my waist, the cocoon of his warmth against my back.

I fold myself down into a cracked leather chair and scrub a hand over my face. "Why does this seem more exhausting than it did yesterday?"

"I know why." Sabh's eyes gleam with wickedness.

"I do too." Meghan gleefully adds.

The three of us have been combing through the sources in the oldest part of the library. When I told them this is where I found the diary, they insisted we needed to thoroughly catalog it. Because if it contained the diary, it could contain other answers. Specifically, curse-defeating, prophecy-nullifying answers.

"If you're both so wise..."

"It's more exhausting today because you didn't spend the night sleeping." Meghan's comment is sly.

"You have rosy cheeks. Like you've been up to things like reconciliation."

When Sabh chimes in I give them an arch look. "And what if we have?"

Meghan's grin is blinding. "Not that we needed confirmation."

"No, we didn't. Hearing my brother laugh again, real laughter, and not laughter full of sarcasm, was confirmation enough."

"He is once again becoming the man I fell in love with."

"Callum said Eachann was always the easiest to love. Did he tell you they used to call him cailin ban?"

Sabh bursts into laughter. "We did! Golden girl. Because women were always following him around, begging to touch and plait his hair."

I'm astonished. "And he let you call him that?"

She shrugs. "There was nothing he could do to stop us."

Meghan looks pensive. "I don't think it was only because of that golden hair. I think it's because he used to laugh a lot. Because he was the one that kept Callum and Carrig from becoming too dour. Callum told me he was always playing practical jokes on them."

"I'll never forget the time he let loose a jar of wee spiders in your mate's boots. I don't know whether he's told you or not, but Callum is deathly afraid of them."

"He hasn't told me that."

Sabh braces her elbows on her knees. "He's probably embarrassed and desperate to forget that particular incident and the way he squealed. He probably hopes no one else remembers it."

I can't imagine my wolfish brother-in-law squealing. "How did he react?"

She starts cackling. "They were skittering over the floor and because he was barefoot and couldn't stomp on them, he made Carrig chase them around the room with his sword."

"Why wasn't my mate the one chasing them?"

"He was standing on the sofa so he was out of the way. He told Carrig that if he found even one spider in his sheets, there'd be hell to pay."

Meghan and I join in her laughter. Because we can both see it. Callum's scowl because of a contrived spider infestation.

"What was Eachann the most afraid of?" My mate has yet to share things like this with me. He told me many stories about this place and his family, but he rarely talked about himself.

"Eachann was always afraid he'd never hear music again."

"He told me he always wanted to be a bard."

Sabh nods. "He always had a harp strapped to his back or tucked under his arm. Until he and Callum turned nine and Father handed them swords. He put the harp away and I never saw him with it again. He may be a warrior now, but his heart's never been in it. He was a poet and a bard first."

Meghan's gaze is troubled. "There's a music room here. I've seen it."

"He won't go anywhere near it. When he put the harp away, something behind his eyes went quiet."

"Did your father forbid him from making music?" If his harp brought him so much joy, how could he so easily walk away from it?

"I don't think so. I think it was his choice."

"But why did he choose it?"

"It's a mystery. If you want answers, you'll have to pry them out of him."

I stand and brush my dusty hands on my jeans. "I may just do that."

"Same time and place tomorrow for our rendezvous?" Meghan proposes.

"Yes. The answer's here. We just have to find it."

I agree with Sabh. We're going to find it. Because I don't want to lose him again.

"Do you remember the song you sang to me when we found the byre at Bealtaine?"

His smile doesn't reach his eyes. "Aye. I wanted you to have music in your head besides that dreadful selkie tale you were so fond of. I have many fond memories of that Bealtaine celebration.

"You never told me where it came from. Did you compose it?"

"It was the last song I set to paper."

"Where is it now?"

He taps a knuckle against his forehead. "Locked away in here. I burned the transcription because I couldn't get the notes to capture what I wanted. I was frustrated."

"Will you sing it to me again?"

"I can't. The music's gone. It left the day they slaughtered me. I've been trying to find it again."

"But I've caught you humming. To me and to Mabh. So you still have music. Is it like writer's block?"

"What's that?"

"It's something Meghan said when I asked her why our favorite author hadn't released any new books in over a decade. She said sometimes writers have all these words in their heads, but the words are just stuck there. She said it was like peanut butter of the mind, whatever that means."

"I don't know what peanut butter is, but aye, it feels like the notes are stuck. I know they're in there somewhere, but I can't hear them."

"Do you think you'll ever hear them again?"

"I want to, leannan. I want to sing to you again. I want to sing to the babe when you grow round with my seed."

"Is there anything I can do? I know a poet's heart beats in your chest, mo stoirm."

He smiles wryly. "My grandmother was a siren and a bard. The first female each uisge bard. I followed her around because the music was like magic to me. She finally got tired of tripping over me and taught me everything she knew."

"Why did you stop making music?"

"Not long after she passed, my father handed me a sword. She was gone, and when you've only nine summers, it can be hard to find a place for your sorrow. It was easier to wield my sword than coax notes from my harp."

"And that wasn't the last of your sorrow."

He rolls over and crosses his arms beneath his head. "No. I should have armor against it. But I don't. When I believed you'd betrayed me..."

"I've finally managed to convince you it wasn't my words that led to the ambush?"

"Aye. We'll probably never know who leaked the information. I keep telling myself it doesn't matter because we still got to this place."

I slide my hand down his chest and trace the whorls of hair at his navel. "And what is this place?"

He circles my wrist and tugs it down. He's already aroused.

"This place is ours. The one we should have had then. And we're going to hoard every single second of it against the darkness we know is coming."

I stroke the silky length of him. "Let's make some moments to hoard, prince."

"King," he corrects me as he tangles his hand in my hair and cups my nape.

"Fine. King." I agree just before my lips find his.

My womb once again swells with his seed.

There is no reason for joy. It means it is the beginning of the end. Once our babe is born he'll set his dagger to my throat and watch me sink below the waves. Despite our reconciliation. Despite how he feels. He believes in the prophecy – even if I do not.

My breasts are tender, and I won't be able to hide the proof of our activities for much longer. I remember his reaction to the news the first time. How he laughed so joyously it made me feel like I was touching the sun. How he swung me in his arms and looked at me like I was a miracle.

How our first babe felt like a beginning, and this babe will mean our end.

He's standing at the window, a mug of coffee in his hand. His back is to me, so I don't have to look in his eyes. It gives me courage.

"I've seen the way you look at Mal and Mabh. I know you're thinking of the child we lost when you hold them."

He turns to face me. "You are the last person I would share that sorrow with."

"When I am the only one who can understand it? When it was my own body that betrayed me? I am the only one you should share it with."

"Any feelings of doubt I held are gone. That is not why I refuse to share it."

"I need you to share it. Because history is repeating itself. And our child will not know his mother for very long."

He inhales, and his expression is unreadable. "You are carrying my child again and I should be full of joy. But the birth of our child means I am that much closer to losing you."

"But we will make the most of every moment. And we'll comb every dusty shelf in the library for a way to thwart the prophecy."

He sighs heavily. "You are certain? We've only been reconciled a fortnight."

I shrug. "Your seed is potent. Once was all it took the first time as well."

"I don't refuse to share the burden of my sorrow because I resent you, leannan. I refuse to share it because I don't wish to heap more sadness on you. And now that we've fulfilled part of the prophecy, our time grows even shorter and you'll know sorrow again. I'll understand if you no longer wish to share my bed. Is this your way of telling me you no longer wish to do so?"

"I still want to share your bed. I won't spend what little time we have left without feeling your touch. Or your kiss. Or the way you wrap your arms around me when the nightmares come."

Chapter Thirty-Seven

Eachann

I've lost it so many times, I'm afraid to tell anyone I found it again. Even my mate. Our child resting in her womb knows. My music is the only thing that soothes him to sleep at night. I wait until my wife drifts away, her hands loose and twitching at her sides, before I begin what has become one of my secret joys.

The song started as four discordant notes that kept repeating themselves in my head. A litany I couldn't escape that was like the cadence of a drumroll. Those notes are the underlying rhythm of the whatever the symphony I'm building will become. When I laid my ear against her stomach and heard our babe's heartbeat for the first time, the melody began to weave its way through those four notes.

It's the story of us. For the babe. The introduction is a run in quarter time that's a hop and skip of notes. Like the sound the brook makes as it trips over rocks on its way to the sea. Like the sound of the tralala selkie song my wife was once so fond of. When I close my eyes and tap out the flow of it, I can almost see the way my grandmother's gnarled hands would dance across the strings if she were still here, her face sharp with glee. It's the wonder of the first time I saw my son's mother – how the brightness was too much to describe with words. The way it struck me and rendered me witless and speechless. How it seeped like sunlight into my soul and chased away the tattered strands of darkness.

I'm still working on the middle part. Because I don't want to shy away from showing the architecture of what happened and how he came to be here in this time so different from my own. I want the core of the symphony to be more than an exposition of sorrow and tragedy.

I borrowed the melody from the composition I played for her in the grove. When I stopped fighting the way I feel, the words were slowly restored to me. And I remembered how her eyes sparkled the first time I called her my wild heart.

"You found your music."

I raise my head and smile sheepishly down at her. "Aye. It settles the babe and your sleep is less troubled when he isn't trying to kick through your stomach."

"Meghan told me each uisge babes grow uncommonly fast, but I didn't realize they grew this fast. I went from carrying around a beachball to hauling a watermelon everywhere I go."

I place my palm on the mound of her stomach and tip her chin up. "A beautiful, ripe, healthy watermelon."

She giggles. "You're ridiculous."

"But I'm your favorite kind of ridiculous." I stroke her cheek. "I am happy, mo chridhe. I didn't know I could be so happy and so full of sorrow and dread at the same time."

Callum and I are sampling the latest batch of whiskey and it gives me the courage to ask about he and Meghan's part in the prophecy. "When did you know the prophecy wasn't about you and Meghan?"

"I didn't know until after I killed her." His confession is raw and hoarse, like it's being torn from his throat.

"But she's here."

"She's here because the sea goddess Cliodhna intervened."

Will Cliodhna intervene on behalf of my mate as well? "How?"

"I held her in my arms and she told me goodbye and asked me to love and teach our son. She said I was a good father and I could tell him how much his mother loved him. Then she told me she was ready because she was doing it for all of us. Because she wanted us to be safe and happy and if that's what came of her death it was more than worth it. So I did it." He takes a deep breath. "I killed her." His voice throbs with the weight of sadness and regret. "I watched the blood well from the line I drew across her throat. I watched the bright red drops scatter over the surface of the blue water as she sank beneath the waves. I was halfway back to shore when I heard her singing. It was Mal's favorite lullaby. And when I turned back around, my eyes were squeezed shut because I was afraid my mind was playing tricks on me. And then she wrapped her arms around me and I knew she wasn't a hallucination."

His whole body trembles at the memory and he swipes tears from the corners of his eyes. "And I'll never again do anything to jeopardize what we have."

"I am happy for you brother."

He hears the sorrow in my tone. "Don't give up hope, brother. The gods may intervene on your behalf when the time comes, just as they did for me."

Chapter Thirty-Eight

Galanta

"**S**top pacing back and forth, brother. You're making me dizzy."

"Ignore him," Carrig rumbles. "You should've seen the state he was in when his mate was delivering Mal."

Their bickering makes me laugh, even through the haze of pain.

"Do you want him in here instead of out there?"

Eachann's great-aunt insisted it was tradition for the men to stay in the antechamber and occupy themselves with cigars and whiskey. Meghan said it sounded like some stupidly archaic thing from one of her bodice rippers.

"Is it allowed?" I'm still learning all the taboos that permeate each uisge culture. If having my mate here while I give birth to our son will somehow generate a thousand-year curse, I won't risk it.

Meghan smiles. "Yes, it's allowed. Callum was there the whole time I was in labor with Mabh. And don't forget you're wed to the king. He can change the rules if they're not to his liking."

"Then, yes please."

"Callum," she shouts. "Send your brother in."

He flings the door open and bounds toward me. He's carrying his harp.

"You brought your harp."

He kneels beside the bed and wipes the tears from my eyes with the pad of his thumb. "I thought it would help soothe you and the babe."

I grab his hand. "It will. But are you sure it's okay if they hear you?"

He hid the fact his music was back. Until our son kicked my stomach so hard it woke me up and I caught him crooning. His favorite thing to do is lay his head there and do a set of every single lullaby he knows, and some he's written himself.

I know the fact it came back to him is still new and fragile and he's very private about it. I don't think he's even shared it with his brother.

He nods. "No singing, just the harp. According to Callum, I'll be required to say things like *you've got this* and *you're a queen* and *I'm right here and I'm not going anywhere*. And possibly I'll be required to agree with you and say *it's all my fault*."

I laugh and then wince when it triggers a contraction. After I breathe my way through it, I loosen my hold on his hand.

The half-moon circles of my nails left imprints across his knuckles, and I kiss them. "Sorry," I murmur.

He presses a kiss to my forehead. "I'm used to the way you like to mark me, witch." He whispers wickedly in my ear. I'd swat him, but another contraction starts rippling through me.

"Push, Galanta! I can see his head." Meghan's crouched at the foot of the bed, waiting to catch him. She and Arianrhod have been with me the whole time.

My mate wraps his hand around mine and I push with all my might. My womb spasms and then I hear him. The volume escalates and Eachann and I share a smile. Meghan clips the umbilical cord, gives him a brisk toweling, and sets him in my arms.

He's completely bald except for a tiny tuft of blond on the crown of his head that's sticking straight in the air. His tiny hands and feet are wrinkled and there's a slight blue tinge to his skin. He's the most beautiful thing I've ever seen.

Eachann holds out his thumb and his son curls his fist around it. "You already have a strong grip, don't ye laddie?"

I love it when his brogue slips out because he's excited. "A strong grip and beautiful turquoise skin."

"It will begin fading in a few days mate, until it's gone completely. It means he is a Son of Lir and carries a beast inside him."

"What shall we call the newest Son of Lir? I'm sure you have ideas. I've seen you poring over all the old bard's tales."

"We could choose one from there, but I had something else in mind."

"Tell me."

"I want to name him after my father. Bhaltair."

I know he had his father's blessing before the end, and that the king was eager to be a grandsire when Eachann told him of the first pregnancy.

"Then Little Bhaltair it is."

Chapter Thirty-Nine

Eachann

Callum, Carrig and I are partaking of the cigars my brother assured me would settle my nerves. Becoming a new father is not for the faint of heart, and though I was barely hanging onto what little composure

I had left when they finally allowed me in the birthing chamber.

I know there will be sleepless nights and my world will be wrung out and turned upside down. I look forward to every piece of it and I am going to find a way to have it all with my mate. I cannot raise my knife against her – not when I have already caused her so much pain. Not when doing so will irrevocably alter me. This time into nothing more than a shadow. And shadows cannot be strong for their children.

I'm tossing back my third glass of whiskey and watching Callum and Carrig wager who can blow the biggest smoke rings, when there's a knock at the door.

"No rest for the wicked," Callum snickers. "Thank the gods and goddesses you're the one always being interrupted now."

I glare at him. "I should place you on the midnight watch."

"Enter."

The door swings open and Riordan strides into our enclave. "I know you're a new father, but I have urgent news."

I hand him a tumbler of whiskey because he looks like he could use it. "I am ready to hear it."

"We've found out who was behind the attack."

"We?"

His jaw tightens. "Me and Langihwen."

"You decided to work with her?"

"She gave me no choice. She refused to leave or abandon her ruse." He's scowling now.

"Who's behind the attacks?"

"It's just as you suspected. They were carried out at the behest of the Kraken King."

"Why? While we don't agree with his ploy for world domination, we have never had a personal quarrel with him or his kingdom."

"This isn't because he has a quarrel. It's because he has his sights set on the throne. He thinks if he eliminates you and Callum and your sons he has a clear line of sight."

"What about Sabh? I'm sure if there were no males of our line to inherit, an exception would be made."

"Exactly. A queen in need of a king. And who better to assume the role of her husband than the man she grew up with? Who also just happens to be the only heir to the Kraken dynasty?"

"He wanted me killed because I stood in the way of a fictitious union between my sister and his son?"

"According to our sources, yes."

"So the attacks will continue?"

"Yes, unless we give him something he wants."

Carrig steps through the doorway, a resigned expression on his face. "He wants me, doesn't he? He wants me to go to him with my tail between my legs and pledge my allegiance to his kingdom instead of this one."

Riordan's gaze is wary. "Yes. I think that would satisfy him."

"If that is what it takes to keep my friends and their families safe, I will do it."

"We can defend ourselves. You don't need to make this sacrifice. You are part of my family too, even if we don't share blood."

He shakes his head. "No. This is what he wants. And I have a godson I want to see grow to manhood. Even if it's from afar. I'll send him word and make arrangements to leave after the sacrifice. You'll need me to help you prepare for it."

Each uisge colts grow fast. According to Callum, Meghan weaned Mal at one month. That's all the time I'll get to make memories that must last me an eternity. The sacrifice must happen once our babe no longer needs his mother's milk.

I'll need him my brother and my friends to lean on once she's gone too, but Carrig thinks appeasing his father will better serve my kingdom. "I know you think you don't have a choice."

"I don't. Not right now. Not when he's so determined to get to me however he can."

"What will you tell Sabh?"

"I'll tell her the same thing I'm telling you. I have to do this to keep all of you safe from his reach."

"You know that won't be enough for her."

His gaze is bleak. "It will have to be. Because I can give her nothing else."

After he bows and exits, I turn to Riordan. "I know I can't stop him from doing this. But find out everything you can about the Kraken court. Use my aunt's network as liberally as your own. There has to be a way to resolve this that won't require his departure."

"I saw Langihwen in the kitchens when I went to fetch a bottle. Have she and Riordan returned?"

"Yes. Apparently his powers of persuasion were weaker than he thought."

She adjusts our son in her arms, and I lean forward to kiss both their foreheads. "Why did he need persuasive powers?"

"Langihwen refused to leave the Kraken court or abandon her disguise until she'd gathered enough information."

"Your shadow master doesn't seem like the kind of man who'd take quietly take direction from a mere girl."

"I don't know the whole story, but she's at least a millennia old. A girl by each uisge standards, but a woman as well. I think he's more than halfway to infatuation."

My mate laughs delightedly. "It's always the ones who think they are invincible that fall the hardest."

"I wouldn't necessarily say Riordan thinks he's invincible."

"Then he obviously doesn't brag about his exploits."

"His exploits? We're all aware of how many times he's saved the kingdom."

"Those aren't the kind of exploits I'm talking about."

I snort. "No. He never mentions those. He's extremely close-mouthed about his amorous encounters. No matter how hard we try to pry the details out of him."

"Well, the women mention them. Frequently and often. He has quite the stable."

I don't bother hiding my surprise. "A stable?"

"Yes, a stable. Sometimes there's a schedule and sometimes it's all of them at once."

"I never suspected. I wonder if my brother and Carrig know?"

"If they did, you know they wouldn't be able to resist teasing him and gossiping about it."

"Men do not gossip."

"That is an absolute falsehood. Men gossip far worse than women. Especially when they've been drinking."

Chapter Forty

Eachann

My wife weaned our son three days ago when he began crawling. His each uisge blood is rising to the surface, because he's growing far more rapidly than a human child. He's already pushing the firetruck around the floor that his cousin Mal gave him and making *vroom vroom* sounds my mate said he got from some Disney movie all the kids are obsessed with.

My mate will never see him take his first step. She'll never hear him say mama or put a band-aid on his knee when he bangs it up because he's chasing after the older cousin who is clearly an object of hero worship.

I want to howl at the gods and drown myself in whiskey. Because the us that we have made will end tomorrow.

I will lose her at my own hand. But tonight I'll finally show her, with all the words she's been asking for, what losing her will mean.

When I ascend the dais, the audience becomes so quiet you can hear the individual breath of every single one of them. My harp stands in the center of the platform, a halo of light skating across the floor surrounding it. The rest of the stage is in shadow, and when I take my seat behind the instrument, I know no one beyond the front row will see anything but the outline of my body curved over around it.

She's in the front row because I want her to see the music on my face as I play and know it is for her. She's holding Bhal in her lap. Her arms are wrapped tightly around him, and his head is resting against her shoulder. The leaf-green eyes she gave him are fastened on me and he's clutching one of the fire trucks Mal gave him. I hope Galanta removed the batteries.

"I've lived a very long time. But I don't think it shows."

There's a ripple of laughter.

"And I've learned a lot of things. But I didn't truly understand what love was or what it meant until I came to know my mate for the second time." I pause to let the words sink in. So she has no doubts about how deeply she is etched into every scar and atom of me. "The first time I fell in love with her, our moments were stolen and our time was short. The second time I fell in love with her, this time, our moments haven't merely been stolen. We've wrested them from the jaws of fate. This time, we know what sacrifices are required and how our story will end."

My fingers lightly caress the harp. "This song is a love letter to my wife. You could say I've been unconsciously writing it for over a thousand years and you wouldn't be wrong. Galanta, this is for you. *Mo chridhe fiadhaich. Wild heart of fire, wild soul of the wood that tames my beast. Mo chridhe fiadhaich, with eyes of green darkness and skin of snow and sunshine. Mo chridhe fiadhaich, I claim your wild heart. I claim your green darkness. I ask you to claim my beast. Mo chridhe fiadhaich, you are my greatest regret, because we wasted time. Mo chridhe fiadhaich, you are the one I will carry in my heart forever, until the last hour. And in my last hour, as my bones turn to coral, and my eyes to sea and sky, I will think only of you and the story of us. Our story that was stolen from us.*

The audience is quiet except for the sound of sniffling and muffled sobs. My mate is clutching our son to her chest, her nose buried in the tuft of hair at the crown of his head.

When I step off the stage and move toward her, she bites her lip. Her tears drip down her chin and slide over her shirt and onto our son. The vines that showed up under her sigil after she saved me are weaving their way up her arms. I pull her into my embrace and she rests her forehead against my chest. I let her tears soak my shirt.

When she starts hiccupping, I tip her chin up. "We were never meant to be a tragedy. But even as we become one, know that this is my music. You are my music."

She nods through her tears. "I know you'll take the best care of him. And promise me that if this is all the hair he grows you'll at least let him have a cool mohawk. And give him my pendant. So he has something of me."

"I promise, mo chridhe fiadhaich."

Chapter Forty-One

Galanta

Our progression to the cove in the half-light of dawn
is solemn. We all thought we would find a way
to prevent another sacrifice. The last few days we have
scoured and pored over every single book and scroll in the

library. Sabh said she wanted to finish her cataloging and recruited us all to help her. But we knew the truth. It was a final collective act of desperation.

The tight grip Meghan and Sabh have on my hands is the only thing keeping me upright. When I placed my son in the arms of his great-great-aunt and kissed his forehead, I wanted to crumble to the floor. When he reached toward me, I let his tiny fist curl around my fingers and raised it to my lips. So memories of the sweet scent of him would give me the strength I needed. Because I do this for him.

The steep trail from the headland to the sandy cove spirals into the mist. I can't see the end of it, but I know he'll be there waiting. There is one part of our story that will remain the same. He will be the one to ease me into the darkness. The last touch I feel, the last gaze I meet. It is the one thing I wanted when I thought I was dying in the grove in a pool of blood. His arms around me and his voice in my ear. His eyes full of the love we were never meant to feel.

This last trek to the bottom is mine alone. Every member of the kingdom stands on this cliff to bear witness, but what happens will only be between the two of us.

When my feet touch the sand, he's there waiting for me. His palm open.

He pulls me toward him, and only sky and sea are reflected in the blue of his gaze. His hold on me is tight, as if he will never let go. When we both know he must.

He tips my chin up, and his gaze is bright with the sheen of unshed tears. "We were never meant to be a tragedy. And I vow, mo chridhe fiadhaich, my green girl, my sweet, savage witch, this is not our ending. I will find you if I must crawl on my knees to the gods and drag you back with the power of the music you gave back to me. Just as Orpheus sought out Eurydice."

The ragged edge of his oath splinters through me. "I will wait for you. I will always wait for you."

He leads me into the water, until I am half-submerged. He anchors me at the waist and tips me over his arm. The gentle lap of the waves cocoons us as he drops his head for the final time.

Because I know this will be our last kiss, I hold nothing back. I want him to know he is enough. That none of this is his fault and I know and understand and accept it.

"Berries," he murmurs when he lifts his head and strokes my bottom lip.

A single tear slides down his cheek and I reach up to catch it on the tip of my thumb. "Jam," I remind him.

He laughs softly. "Only you would remind me of joy in a moment like this, leannan."

"I do this for you. For our son. Find joy in that, because I do. I know that my death will bring peace to our kingdom."

He closes his eyes, but tears still leak from the corners. I feel the tracks of salt on my own face as well. His arm trembles when he raises the dagger.

I let go of everything but the love I feel.

"Drop the knife, prince. She is not meant to be your sacrifice."

The voice is one I know well. My gaze snaps to his in astonishment and we turn in unison to confront the Morrigan.

She is in her fierce reaper form, garbed in battle leathers, a raven perched on each shoulder.

"I do not enjoy repeating myself."

My mate flings the blade. It arcs through the mist and embeds itself in one of the craggy rocks near the beach.

"I am disappointed in you, little witch. You gave up too soon. The darkness coming for this island will only be defeated if all of you work together. That is what the prophecy meant."

"But it hasn't been fulfilled." My mate protests.

"Where do you think prophecies come from, King? Do you think they're spun out of thin air? They are not. We create them. And it has now been twice fulfilled. Your mate met the terms of it in my grove over a thousand years ago."

He turns back to me then. The tears are full of wonder instead of sorrow this time. "The story of us isn't over."

I don't know what the future will bring because the goddess's explanation sounded ominous. I do know that even though the darkness is coming I'll be here so we can fight it together.

I rise to my toes to kiss him. "No, it isn't over. It's just beginning."

Langihwen

“If you do this, you'll be the target of his anger.” I'm speaking to my reflection because I have no one else

I can make my confession to. No one else to talk me out of my idiocy. This court is dangerous. And acting the part of a lady's maid and avoiding all the roving hands has been a challenge. The kraken men have been known to take what they want – whether or not it's freely offered. So far I've managed to evade the clutches of the worst lechers and have only been forced to endure mild groping. I just grit my teeth and pretend I'm flattered when I'm anything but. When what I really want to do is humiliate them with my knife.

I know the spymaster won't tolerate another man's hands on me like that. Even though he pushed himself away when our sparring became too intense and he almost kissed me.

Although Riordan is the one who trained me, he doesn't trust my abilities. I've been refining my skills for over a hundred years and he has yet to send me on a single mission. His coddling is why I finally approached my aunt.

Aunt Arianrhod's network is an unofficial one, but its reach is vast and stretches across the globe. If this mission is a success, it will be the first step to earning a reputation as one of the kingdom's most cunning spies. There's only one problem.

The spymaster followed me here. I don't know if he was sent here by the king or if he followed me because he thinks

I'm incapable of finishing this task without bungling it or ending up dead or maimed. I saw right through his disguise. He's too arrogant to pass for a firestarter. He painted soot across his face, and I saw the grit beneath his nails, but he couldn't wipe that telltale smirk away when he saw me.

I smirked right back and stood my ground. I am not going to let him tow me home like a recalcitrant child.

Acknowledgements

I couldn't write about HEAs if I didn't have one of my own. To my husband- who's okay with peanut butter sandwiches when I'm on a deadline, and always remembers to hang up the laundry.

To every one of you who's the icing on the cake and keeps me smiling – you know who you are. I'd ride at dawn for you just like you would for me.

To the Willow Creek Wantons – you make this all worthwhile! And especially to Sacha – thank you from the bottom of my heart for everything you do!

Last, but not least, to all of the arc readers and book bloggers and booktubers and bookish podcasts. Thank you for sharing your love of indie authored books. We see you and we appreciate you.

About the author

It all started when I read Bard: Odyssey of the Irish in the 8th grade. I was immediately obsessed with Celtic mythology and Irish and Scottish folklore. I still have the huge coffee table tome entitled *The Celts* that was my most anticipated sixteenth birthday gift.

Kresley Cole and Karen Marie Moning only amped up my fascination with paranormal romance with Immortals After Dark and the Fever series. Both series have elements of Celtic mythology and epic fantasy I wanted to explore.

I've always wanted to write paranormal romance grounded in myth and historical fantasy, and I finally get to do that with The Sons and Daughters of Lir.

For the warrior hearts and the poet souls.

Listen to the Official Playlist

My Website

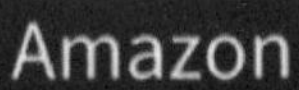

Amazon

Social Media

www.ingramcontent.com/pod-product-compliance
Lightning Source LLC
Chambersburg PA
CBHW021842130726
47989CB00009B/3056